# THE HAUNTING

# The Haunting

Lindsey Duga

Scholastic Inc.

ISBN 978-1-338-50651-8

10 9 8 7 6 5 4 3 2 1    20 21 22 23 24

Printed in the U.S.A. 40
First printing 2020

Book design by Stephanie Yang

TO MOM:
THERE WILL ALWAYS BE
"JUST ONE MORE CHAPTER."

The wrought iron bars of the fence surrounding Evanshire's Home for Neglected Girls were slick with that evening's rain, and chilled by the fog. Even so, Emily wrapped her hands tightly around them, ignoring the cold wetness, and let out a soft whistle through her teeth.

She waited patiently, as she did every night, for her best friend. But she didn't have to wait long. Almost immediately, a four-legged creature trotted forward in the gloom, its existence made visible only by the dim gas streetlamps above. It emerged from behind a tower of old shipping crates, looking more like a shadowy monster from another world than a slender canine from the streets of London.

As the dog approached the fence, Emily could tell her friend Archie had gotten into even more trouble that day than yesterday, or the day before that. His fine brown-and-white coat was muddy, and his white paws were covered in black soot, as if he'd decided to crawl his way through the inside of a chimney like Simon, the tall, balding chimney sweep who came to the orphanage every month.

Emily held out her fingers through the bars and Archie licked them eagerly, his tongue lingering on her sore red knuckles as though he somehow knew the injury was for his benefit. How he knew, Emily had no idea. Dogs were just smart that way.

Because the rapping on Emily's knuckles *had* been for Archie's sake. At supper, she'd swiped a small piece of meat pie off her own plate, and while she managed to hide it in the pocket of her smock, Miss Evanshire saw the trail of crumbs across the table and assumed—rightly—that Emily was to blame for the mess. Miss Evanshire had rapped Emily's knuckles with her cane and warned the girl that rats could be sent into her bed once they'd had enough of her crumbs.

But rats didn't scare Emily; the thought of not being able to see Archie did.

He whined and sniffed the girl's wrists while she scratched behind his ears. "Shhh, boy, quiet now." With her other hand she pulled out the smooshed meat pie and held it out through the bars. "Eat up, I've got to get to bed before someone notices I'm gone," she whispered, more to herself than to Archie, as he always had a habit of scarfing down his meal instead of savoring every bite.

Sure enough, the English pointer mutt finished his dinner in two gulps, hardly chewing the mushy, soft pastry. Emily bent down, her face pressed against the bars, arms threaded through them, and hugged her friend around his ashen neck. Her smock was dirty enough that no one would question the soot stains later.

How Emily wished she could give Archie a real hug and

play fetch, but she hadn't been able to do that for a year now. Not since he'd gotten too big to easily pass through the fence, and Emily had to make sure that he wasn't inside the grounds of Evanshire, lest he be caught by one of the caretakers—or worse, the old witch herself. So she'd let him out through the fence one day, knowing that, as dangerous as the streets of London were, at least out there he had a chance, while under Miss Evanshire's nose he would surely be sent to the pound.

Like Emily, Archie had no parents. He had been abandoned, just as she had. Except she'd found him in a shipping crate one day when she'd passed the docks on the way back from mass, whereas a constable had discovered a newborn Emily under a bench in Regent's Park. Emily had taken the shivering, tiny puppy and hid him in her coat. By some miracle she had managed to keep him hidden until he'd gotten too big for the attic, then too big to slip through the fence.

But even after she'd taken Archie outside the gate, he hadn't abandoned her. He came back every night, even when there was no food to share several evenings in a row.

Archie did his best to lick away any final crumbs on her hands, his slippery pink tongue darting between her fingers to grab every last morsel.

"Good boy," she murmured softly, stroking his neck and looping around to scratch under his chin. Archie's soft brown eyes grew sleepy and content as he enjoyed her touch, until Emily finally had to pull away. "I'll be back tomorrow," she told him, as she did every night.

Reluctantly, and with one final look at the dog she'd raised since he was a little pup, Emily ducked under the hedges and crawled through the bushes of rhododendrons, their strong scent tickling her nose. Praying she wouldn't sneeze, Emily scrambled to her feet and stuck to the shadowy corners of the grounds until she came to the back door. It was ajar and creaked loudly on its rusty hinges. She was confident, though, that no one would hear.

It was just before curfew, around the time when the groundskeeper, Mr. Duford, would be having a "special drink," as he liked to call it, in the scullery. Emily didn't say anything about his drink and he didn't say a word about her using the back door so late. It was an unspoken mutual understanding between them.

She took the stairs two at a time and hurried down the hall, avoiding the floorboards that made the most noise, and finally slipped into the dormitory that she shared with five other girls.

"You're in trouble," came a singsong voice from the farthest bed, next to the window.

Emily shut the door behind her, nerves spiking as she whirled around and found her second least favorite person sitting on *her* bed. Lying on her stomach, feet in the air, Agatha wore a smug smile on her face.

"Get off my bed," Emily snapped.

"Miss Evanshire already came for the head count, and *you* weren't in your bed."

Emily's stomach shriveled and dropped like a stone.

"But . . . she's early!" Emily protested, as if this fact alone were reason enough that she shouldn't be punished for being out of bed at night.

Agatha raised her eyebrow at the stupidity of the declaration, knowing as well as Emily—and as well as any other girl at the orphanage—that this meant absolutely nothing. "She said she didn't care if you were eaten by rats or taken away by Spring-Heeled Jack," Agatha said, her lips curling into an even bigger, crueler smile.

Emily recoiled at the mention of the slender half devil, half man who was said to roam the streets of London frightening innocent young woman. The very idea of being anywhere near the awful creature with red eyes, who could leap over nine-foot-tall fences, was utterly terrifying.

Miss Evanshire's heartlessness, on the other hand, wasn't at all surprising. Out of all the girls, Emily was the one who the old woman hated most—she was sure of it.

Little Mary, one of the youngest girls, sidled up to Emily, tugging on Emily's sleeve. "She came early to tell us a couple would be coming tomorrow," Mary informed, her green eyes wide and bright. "She said they want to adopt a girl as soon as possible!"

Emily wanted to be as excited and as hopeful as Mary, but she'd long since stopped hoping or dreaming of being adopted. After twelve years in the orphanage, watching couples come and go, taking the prettiest girls with soft curls and big blue eyes, Emily had simply stopped expecting a different, more beautiful life. She knew her future lay in a workhouse. In only a couple short years, she'd leave her little bed in this dank dormitory for an even worse bed in an even drearier room. Bruises, burns, and an empty belly would be her only proof of a long and endless day of work. In fact, her imagination would be all she'd have to keep her mind from going loopy from exhaustion and a never-ending ache in her bones.

But Emily refused to instill in the younger, newer girls the same sense of hopelessness she had, or the same acceptance. So she smiled and placed her hand on Mary's strawberry-blond hair. "That's so exciting."

Agatha gave a very unladylike snort and hopped off Emily's bed. "Don't be daft. They'll do what every couple does. Come to look at us, compare us, throw around fancy words, then leave. Same as always."

Mary's gaze dropped to the floor, the light in her eyes vanishing like the flame on a candlewick.

"Don't worry, tomorrow will be different," Emily whispered in Mary's ear. "I can feel it."

Mary gave Emily a happy, shining, *hopeful* smile, and Emily tried to return it as best as she could, even though the lie twisted, painful and sharp, in her chest.

# 2

The next morning Emily was instructed to go without breakfast—or rather, she was forced. It wasn't anything new, to miss a meal, but having given away a portion of her dinner to Archie the night before, she felt hungrier than usual. But hunger was a thing she was well acquainted with.

The girls were given two bars of soap to share among them to wash up and get ready for the couple, who were on their way. Miss Evanshire seemed especially on edge. She paced the halls like a royal guard, stiff and stern, with the power to make any poor soul suffer if even a pinkie toe was stepped out of line. It was also clear she had done *her* best to impress her guests as well. The woman had even gone so far as to fasten an old brooch to her satin burgundy dress with the high lace collar. Her gray hair was smoothed back in a tight bun, and a bit of rouge had been applied to her lips.

In Emily's opinion, it was a bit like trying to dress up a walking skeleton. Not only was it pointless, it was a little scary, too.

With Miss Evanshire's prodding, the girls were lined up by age and marched down the old—but recently shined—wooden steps toward the parlor. They passed portraits of Miss Evanshire's uncle, the man who had started the orphanage and whose sour disposition had been passed down to his niece and increased tenfold. Everything in the house was old, but cleaned, buffed, and scrubbed, by its young female residents, until it looked like it had been bought yesterday.

"Mary, smooth out your dress," Miss Evanshire barked as soon as they had formed a line in front of the parlor's deep red chintz sofa. "Alice, wash your face again, you look a fright!" When she came to the end of the line, right in front of Emily, she sneered hatefully. "Don't forget to smile, you ungrateful child. You are lucky to get even this chance before your miserable fate is sealed." She batted her cane against Emily's shin, but Emily didn't wince. She didn't like giving Miss Evanshire the satisfaction.

As soon as the old hag's back was turned, Emily stuck out her tongue. Mary, who happened to catch Emily's small act of rebellion, gave her a small, appreciative smile just as a knock sounded at the door. The girls at once began to whisper hurriedly, all of them fidgeting in their best dresses.

All except Emily.

Emily wasn't nervous, because she knew how this would end: The couple would take one look at her dark hair, rough hands, freckles, and brown eyes, and see a girl unsuited for teatime and fancy dresses.

Voices drifted in from the hallway. A deep baritone and

a gentle, melodic voice mingled with Miss Evanshire's annoying croak.

"I think you'll find we have the best-behaved young girls in all of London, Mr. and Mrs. Thornton," Miss Evanshire said loudly in a sickeningly sweet croon, the footsteps coming down the hall toward the parlor, where the eighteen girls awaited nervously.

Emily resisted the urge to roll her eyes. She had to be on her best behavior. She didn't want to miss tea as well.

The couple who walked in were perfect representations of the voices from the entrance hall. A petite blond woman in an olive-green satin gown, tight sleeves accentuating her small, delicate shoulders, walked arm-in-arm with a tall man who had dark hair and a thick mustache, sporting a handsome deep blue suit.

They were absolutely lovely.

In all her time at Evanshire's Home for Neglected Girls, Emily had never seen a more charming, perfect couple.

She could see how rich they were, too. While their posture, their aura, and even their scent reeked of high society, they wore evidence of it as well. Mrs. Thornton's shiny jeweled rings and bracelets. Mr. Thornton's ivory cane and silver chain from a pocket watch hidden within the folds of his smartly tailored suit.

They were too good—too *perfect*—to be true.

Mrs. Thornton was the first to look at the girls, her eyes going from orphan to orphan down the line—until they stopped abruptly at Emily.

Emily dropped her gaze, her cheeks warming. She'd been staring, rather rudely, at Mrs. Thornton, admiring her dress and soft gold curls. But so were the other girls, Emily was sure of it.

"Now, Mr. and Mrs. Thornton, you neglected to mention what age you were looking for, so they are lined up from youngest to oldest, starting from the left. Each girl can read, write, and do arithmetic. They are also taught embroidery and piano and—"

"Robert," Mrs. Thornton's voice cut through Miss

Evanshire's rehearsed speech, as the lady's olive-green skirts swished into Emily's view. "This one."

Eyes widening, Emily peeked from under her dark bangs to see Mrs. Thornton staring down at her, jaw clenched and cheeks pale under a layer of rose-colored powder. The way Mrs. Thornton clutched the pendant on her necklace so hard her knuckles turned white drew Emily's attention to its odd shape. It was long and silver, quite unlike any jewel or ornament Emily had seen before.

In moments, Mr. Thornton joined Mrs. Thornton, and Emily found herself being inspected like a piece of meat at a butcher shop, or perhaps the Queen's crown jewels.

"What is your name, dear?" Mrs. Thornton asked, looking down at the girl before her.

"E-Emily," she stuttered.

Emily's palms broke out in a cold sweat, and she clenched her fists. She chose to keep her attention on the couple's shoes rather than their eyes, which seemed to be targeting each of her flaws.

Soft, gloved fingertips lightly tapped under Emily's chin, pulling her face upward and forcing her to stare into Mrs. Thornton's blue eyes.

"Emily, yes . . ." Mrs. Thornton said, her gaze softening ever so subtly, but her look remaining rather . . . intense. "She's perfect. Don't you think, dear?"

Never in her life had Emily been referred to as perfect. Clearly Mrs. Thornton needed spectacles.

Mr. Thornton nodded. "Yes, darling."

Emily tore her eyes away from Mrs. Thornton and looked beyond the couple to see Miss Evanshire gaping at them. If Emily hadn't been as shocked as the old witch, then she would've taken the opportunity to stick her tongue out at her then, too.

Did this mean . . . after all this time . . . was she really getting adopted?

As if on cue, Mr. Thornton whirled around to Miss Evanshire. "Well, what needs to be drawn up? Does she have any belongings that need to be packed up and taken to the carriage?"

"I . . . well . . . she . . ." Miss Evanshire moved her mouth up and down a few times but no words came out. Finally, she sighed and waved her cane toward the study. "This way, please. If you are certain that you want *that* child"—she layered the disgust onto her words like strawberry jam on an almond scone—"then there is paperwork to be signed."

With a gentle nod at their future adopted daughter, the Thorntons followed Miss Evanshire out of the parlor.

As soon as the adults were gone, the girls broke out into excited whispers while Emily merely stood there in a daze, unsure of what had just happened. Surrounding Emily, they all began congratulating her—all except one.

A hand seized Emily's arm above the elbow, nails digging into her skin. The force of Agatha's grip made Emily wince, and she tried to shake the girl off. "Let go."

"Don't act so conceited," Agatha hissed. "Remember what you'd be leaving behind if you go."

"A lumpy bed, meager meals, a cranky old lady, and a spoiled brat," Emily retorted quickly, her temper rising.

Agatha hadn't been at Miss Evanshire's for very long—only a year or so—but she was older and not likely to get adopted. Agatha had been born into a life of privilege until tax collectors had come for her parents. She saw herself as better than everyone. Certainly better than Emily, who'd never known anything but loneliness, hard work, and misfortune.

Agatha sneered, her pale eyes flashing with evil glee. "Don't forget a skinny, dirty *mutt*."

Emily froze, the blood running cold in her veins as the weight of Agatha's veiled threat fell on her.

Adult voices once again drifted through the hallway.

"What do you think will happen to your precious doggy once you go away? Miss Evanshire will have him sent to the pound as soon as she sees him outside waiting for you." Agatha spoke low and fast as the footsteps neared.

All this time Agatha had known about Archie but kept it to herself—kept it, no doubt, for a moment just like this.

Emily was speechless as Agatha continued to smirk, clearly happy to inflict one more emotional blow before

Emily left for a better, brighter life. But now she couldn't. Maybe that's why Agatha said it—because she knew what Emily's response would be.

All too quickly, the three adults returned and Mrs. Thornton made a beeline to Emily, taking the girl's chilled hand in her gloved ones. "Come, dear. Time to go to your new home."

All her life, Emily had dreamed of those words, and each time she imagined it, she had never said what she was about to say.

"No."

Mrs. Thornton blinked down at Emily. All the girls froze, their lips parting in surprise, while Miss Evanshire stared at her in utter horror and Mr. Thornton looked mildly annoyed.

"I beg your pardon?" Mrs. Thornton asked.

"No, I don't—I'm not going." Her voice trembled at the words, shaky with the threat of tears that were bound to fall from being forced to make this awful choice.

Because she couldn't abandon Archie. She just couldn't.

He was her friend. Her confidant. Her puppy. Not for the possibility of more food, open spaces in the country air, or a better home with a better family. She couldn't abandon him because he had never abandoned her.

Miss Evanshire marched through the crowd of girls and seized Emily by the wrist roughly. "Foolish, ungrateful child—" She seethed, shaking Emily so hard she felt her insides rattle.

"Miss Evanshire, please!" Mr. Thornton barked, storming forward and steering Emily away from the grasp of the older woman. "Perhaps we should speak to the child alone for a moment."

Red-faced, from either anger or embarrassment, Miss Evanshire shooed the rest of the girls out of the parlor, snarling at them and batting the backs of their calves with her cane.

Once she was alone with the Thorntons, Emily had a hard time keeping from bursting into tears. Somehow she kept them back, though her chin trembled. Mr. Thornton sighed, crossing to the door, grumbling under his breath, making his large mustache quiver, while Mrs. Thornton knelt before Emily, a small, gentle smile on her pink lips.

"Why do you not want to come with us, Emily?" Mrs. Thornton's voice was soothing and sweet, and ever so tempting. "We could give you a great big house to play in and pretty dresses to wear."

"M-my friend can't come." Emily swallowed, her words growing steadier with her resolve. She was *not* leaving Archie.

Mrs. Thornton frowned. "Who's your friend?"

"Archie."

She frowned deeper, eyebrows pulling together in confusion. "But . . . there are only girls here."

Emily bit her lip, about to spill her biggest secret. But she could trust Mrs. Thornton, couldn't she? After all, the woman was asking to become her new mother. Didn't that mean Emily should trust her?

She took a deep breath and said in a rush, "Archie is my dog. He lives outside the fence. And if I leave, Agatha will tell Miss Evanshire, and he will be sent to the pound!"

"A dog!" Mrs. Thornton cried, her gloved hand flying to her chest, then clumsily grasping the metal pendant about her neck. After a moment, she smiled, relieved. "Well, perhaps something can be arranged. Dear?"

She looked over her shoulder at her husband, who stood behind her, watching Emily with an unreadable expression.

"A dog, hmm?" he said, his fingers stroking the tips of his mustache and clean-shaven jaw. "Charlotte, darling, are you sure . . ." His words trailed off at his wife's pleading look. He sighed again and, to Emily's utmost surprise, gave her a gentle pat on the head. "All right, where is this dog of yours?"

The carriage ride out of London was all a blur. The entire time, Emily could scarcely believe her fortune. She kept wondering which bump in the road would be painful enough to jar her out of this beautiful dream, but the horses trotted on, and the smokestacks and brick apartments of sprawling London fell away to reveal a rolling countryside that Emily had seen only a few times in her life.

She found herself leaning out the window, smelling the fresh air, feeling the breeze on her cheeks, and hearing Archie's panting in the back of the carriage, where the

Thorntons' footman had boarded him in a crate for the journey.

Mr. Thornton wouldn't allow the dog inside the carriage, and Emily had nothing to bring with her except Archie, so he took the place of where her luggage would've been. When Emily had tried packing the two meager dresses she owned, Mrs. Thornton had *tsk*ed and handed them back to Miss Evanshire, saying, "We'll find you something much more . . . suitable, my dear." Emily was sure she'd never forget the look of offense on the old woman's face.

Getting Archie to come hadn't been hard at all. She had whistled and he had bounded toward her, tongue hanging out. Licking and placing his paws on her chest, whining with happiness, the English pointer mix had been overjoyed to see his friend without bars in the way, while the Thorntons leaned away in distaste at his dirty coat. But the Thorntons stayed true to their word and brought the dog along.

And now here was Emily, riding out with her new family, to a new home, a new life.

It was still so hard to believe.

As the sun dipped low in the sky, cresting the English hills and spilling orange and gold light across the fields, Emily couldn't remember ever seeing a more lovely sight. *Nothing can be more beautiful than this,* she thought. And then she was almost immediately proven wrong.

Coming around a bend in the road with tall, wild woods on either side, Emily could just catch a glimpse of something other than nature. As they got nearer, the structure morphed into a majestic stone manor. It extended great, dark silver wings with windows upon windows in neat rows, each one surrounded by thick, curling vines of ivy.

It was magnificent.

Emily was even more shocked to find that the carriage turned down the path toward the building.

"Welcome to Blackthorn Manor, Emily," Mr. Thornton said with a kind smile, patting her knee. "Your new home."

*This?* This was to be her new home?

Blackthorn Manor wasn't a home; it was practically a castle. But in size alone. Unlike the princesses' homes from fairy tales, this seemed to be a home for the characters who lived in the horror novels that Mr. Duford liked to read, like Dr. Frankenstein or Mr. Hyde. A place of history and secrets. Grand, yes, but mysterious. Beautiful, but terrifying.

"It's so . . . big," Emily said, not sure if she could express all that she was feeling other than stating the obvious.

Across the carriage compartment, Mrs. Thornton sighed, looking out the window, her face impossibly sad.

But why?

Emily thought taking home a child that she wanted was supposed to be a happy, good thing, and yet Mrs. Thornton stared out at Blackthorn Manor like it was a prison. A place of grief and loneliness.

Her gloved hand clenched the strange pendant around her neck a little tighter, then fiddled with the chain between her fingertips.

Mrs. Thornton caught Emily staring at her and gave Emily a comforting smile.

Emily returned the smile and quickly looked away,

remembering that it was rude to stare at people. But was it rude when it was one's own mother? She had no idea.

Soon the carriage rolled to a stop in front of the great estate and Emily felt her nerves get the better of her. Now that she was here and it was so close—her home and her future—another worry crept into her mind like a spider.

What if they decided they didn't want her?

What if, a week later, they thought Emily wasn't good enough, pretty enough, or talented enough to call their daughter? Surely the Thorntons would send her back.

Well, Emily decided then and there that she wouldn't return to Evanshire's. She'd go straight to a workhouse. She wasn't going back to the orphanage.

"Emily? Out you get, dear," Mr. Thornton called from outside the carriage, holding out his large hand.

Swallowing, Emily grasped his hand and stepped down from the carriage, hopping the final step. As soon as her old shoes touched the pebbles, she felt a tremor under her feet, the sensation making its way up her knees and to the base of her spine.

Emily's gaze shot up, at first looking to see if Mr. Thornton felt it, too, but seeing instead the manor looming above her—so different than it had appeared mere seconds before. Shadows seemed to slide down the stone walls as the ivy withered and died before her eyes. Every crack and crevice in the stones of the manor looked as if it were bleeding black ink, dripping down to the ground and soaking the grass with darkness and decay. In a second-story window there was a shadowy figure, painted inky black against the glass.

Then Emily blinked, and it was all gone.

The house wasn't dark at all. It was illuminated in the fading light of the setting sun. It made the ivy leaves gleam gold and the stone, somewhat wet from the afternoon rain, shine silver. The windows were clear, and the manor looked every bit like the castle she'd seen through the carriage windows.

So what had she just witnessed?

Too confused to put her thoughts into words, Emily let Mrs. Thornton lead her up the steps while Mr. Thornton and the footman got Archie's crate down from the carriage and opened it.

"We'll let Mr. Frederickson wash up Archie," Mrs. Thornton said as they reached the large door with an ornate iron knocker.

Before Emily's very eyes, the knocker's metal details morphed into a face like that of a gargoyle, complete with horns and fangs and soulless eyes.

Emily froze, too scared to even breathe.

But it was gone in the next instant. Faster than a blink. Like a flash, it had never been there at all.

"Emily?"

"Yes?" Emily squeaked, tearing her eyes away from the knocker. *It was nothing. Just your nerves,* she thought.

"Did you hear me? I said, are you hungry?"

Having missed teatime and been given only a loaf of bread on the ride in, Emily's mouth watered at the mere mention of food. She nodded vigorously and Mrs. Thornton gave her a light, airy laugh. "I'm a bit peckish myself. I do hope Miss Greer has fixed us up something tasty."

Just then the door opened, revealing a woman with a round face framed by curly gray hair. She narrowed her eyes at Mrs. Thornton, then smiled, winking good-naturedly. "Now, Mrs. Thornton, you say something like that and it implies that not *all* my food is tasty."

"Good gracious, how foolish of me! Of course it is *all* delectable, Miss Greer," Mrs. Thornton replied, her gloved hand lightly feathering across her chest in mock surprise.

"That's better! Now"—Miss Greer swiveled toward Emily, hands on her broad hips, mirroring her equally broad stance and frame—"who do we have here?"

"This," Mrs. Thornton said, coming behind Emily and placing her hands on the girl's shoulders, "is Emily. Emily, this is Miss Greer. She is our cook and housekeeper."

Miss Greer bent at the waist to look Emily in the eyes. Miss Greer's eyes were as gray as her hair, accentuated by smile lines and crow's-feet. "Pleasure to meet you,

Miss Emily," she said softly, taking Emily's hand and clasping it between her own much larger, calloused hands.

Remembering her manners, Emily swallowed and gave her a shaky smile. "The pleasure is all mine, Miss Greer." Maybe it was *this* woman she saw in the window, and the creepy shadows were nothing but a trick of the clouds and the sunlight. After all, in the middle of dreary London, the world outside always looked a little paler. Yes, that had to be it.

Behind them a shout echoed across the grounds, and Emily barely had time to turn around before Archie pounced on her. His strong, still-dirty paws dug into her smock while his tail whacked against the shins and dresses of Miss Greer and Mrs. Thornton.

"My word!" Miss Greer exclaimed, grabbing Archie by his neck and hauling him off Emily. "Where did this beast come from?"

"Oh, Miss Greer, he's not a beast—he's my friend!" Emily laughed, taking Archie's face in her hands and smoothing down his ears. Archie immediately calmed at her touch, panting with his pink tongue rolling out and his big brown eyes jumping from Emily to the other two women.

"And why on earth is the friendly beast here?" Miss Greer asked, her gaze shooting pointedly to Mr. Thornton, who was mounting the steps and stripping off his sharp navy coat.

"Emily wouldn't leave without him," Mr. Thornton said.

"I see." Miss Greer pursed her lips, folding her arms over her chest.

Archie whined, licking Emily's fingers, his distress at this new world and the new people coming out through his nervous puppy tics.

Finally, Miss Greer sighed and muttered, "Seems to me there must've been plenty of *other* orphan girls without the extra baggage of a dog."

Emily heard Miss Greer just fine despite her low voice, and Emily felt her face flush with heat. But she couldn't say anything in defense, because it was true. There were probably hundreds of poor orphaned girls in the city of

London without a dog, or who were prettier, smarter, cuter, better educated. Why did it have to be Emily?

"Emily was the only girl who looked—"

Mrs. Thornton stopped abruptly, her hand latching on to the silver pendant at her neck. Her face seemed to rapidly lose its color and became as white as milk. Then her other hand strayed to her forehead, and she said meekly, "Forgive me, I've a headache. I must . . . decline supper."

"Darling." Mr. Thornton reached for his wife, but she waved him off, her olive silk skirts swishing as she hurried beyond the doors and disappeared into the depths of the house.

"Oh, dear," Miss Greer murmured. "I'm sorry, Mr. Thornton, I—"

"It's quite all right, Miss Greer. Let's just have a nice supper. I'm sure Emily is quite hungry. But perhaps you could bring Charlotte some tea later?"

"Of course, sir," Miss Greer said, taking Emily's hand and tugging her into the house.

Mr. Thornton and the footman, Mr. Frederickson,

guided Archie down the steps around the manor, the two men mentioning something about a metal tub and water for washing.

While Emily didn't necessarily want to leave Archie, she knew she was pushing her luck by even having him here in the first place. Silently promising herself that she would check on him later, she allowed herself to be led into Blackthorn Manor by Miss Greer.

Stepping into the hall of Blackthorn Manor really was like entering a castle. Emily hadn't read much about fairy tales or King Arthur and his knights, but some of the girls at the orphanage had told her stories about them.

The castles in fairy tales had sky-high ceilings, marble floors, plush rugs, velvet drapes. They had fine pale blue china and shiny silverware and brass clocks.

Blackthorn had it all. But the feature that reminded Emily the most of a castle was the grand staircase that led to the second floor, with its gorgeous mahogany banister and a crystal chandelier that hung overhead. The setting sun hit the ornate fixture just right to create rainbows that cascaded across the entrance hall.

Miss Greer, however, didn't give Emily much time at all to admire the hall. Instead, she pulled her forward past the staircase and into the west wing, muttering things about mutts, and too much work, and dog hair.

As they passed the foot of the stairs, Emily ran her hand across the banister, her fingers coming away with a thick layer of gray dust. It was then that Emily saw past the grand beauty of the entrance hall and saw the grim details . . .

The dust. The cobwebs. The stale scent in the air.

Emily's first impression of the manor from the outside was more accurate: This was not a castle for princesses, but a castle for monsters.

Dust clung to every surface while cobwebs were strung across the banister and coated the chandelier. In the corners, shadows seemed to crawl along the walls and floors like spiders.

When they reached the scullery, and Miss Greer

instructed Emily to sit at an old wooden table as she hurried to tend to her cooking, Emily knew at once that she preferred the simplicity of eating in the kitchen to a fancy dining room with fine china and trying to remember which fork to use.

All Emily wanted was a hot meal without being too nervous to enjoy the food she was eating, so she was grateful when Miss Greer set a plate in front of her with boiled potatoes, roasted chicken, fresh vegetables, and a small saucer of gravy, without any flourish or finesse. After all, even this was already fancier than what Emily was used to at Evanshire's.

Miss Greer was also too busy to ask Emily anything, so the girl was free to eat as unladylike as she wished, but she was careful not to eat too fast or too much. The last thing she wanted was a stomachache her first night with the Thorntons.

When she'd eaten all she could, Emily pushed her plate away and was about to ask Miss Greer if she could help with anything, when the opposite door opened, revealing a very wet Mr. Thornton, a half-dry—but clean—Archie, and a blooming garden behind them.

Miss Greer gaped at Mr. Thornton while Emily pressed her fist to her mouth, hoping to hide a tirade of giggles at her new adoptive father's sopping wet, now drooping, mustache.

"That"—he took a large breath and, for a moment, Emily was worried that he would yell like Miss Evanshire so often did, but instead his mouth broke into a broad grin, showing white teeth—"was the most fun I've had in a long while. I don't think this boy has ever had a bath before."

Emily shook her head, still surprised that he wasn't furious over his ruined fancy suit. "No, sir."

"Hmm, well, I thought he was going to be troublesome, but he seems like a good chap," Mr. Thornton said, patting the top of Archie's head. "I imagine it will be nice to have him around. Don't you think so, Miss Greer?"

Miss Greer wrinkled her nose, showing her displeasure, but she shrugged and said, "If you say so, sir. I'm about to take up some tea to Mrs. Thornton. Supper is on the stove for you and Mr. Frederickson."

"Thank you, Miss Greer. I'll show Emily to her room now."

"Very good, sir." With that, Miss Greer picked up a tray laden with tea and biscuits and bustled out of the scullery, her curls bouncing as she walked.

Archie trotted over to Emily, and she set down her plate of scraps. The hungry dog quickly gobbled up the remnants of her supper.

"You don't have to do that, my dear. We'll make sure Archie is rightly fed," Mr. Thornton said. "Now, let's get you to your room. You must be tired."

Once again, he held out his hand and Emily took it, a wave of warmth washing through her like she'd never known before. It was the feeling of kindness, of acceptance. Emily wondered how she'd survived without it all these years.

❧

Mr. Thornton took her through the manor, up the grand staircase, and down the second-floor hallway. She noted their footprints indented into the rugs, disturbing the thin layer of dust. *Are all big houses so dusty?* she wondered.

Evanshire's was a big house—granted, not *this* big—but it was immaculate. Then again, the girls had to do all the cleaning. Was it just Miss Greer alone to take care of the place and do all the chores? Emily couldn't imagine shouldering such a big job.

The light fixtures on the walls didn't look any better. They were rusty and layered in yet more dust, and she could see the crevices packed with what looked like mold.

But if you looked beyond the dust (or rather, if you didn't look too carefully), it was still an elegant estate. Fancy curtains and ornate gold frames around expensive-looking paintings. Lovely wall tapestries and small marble sculptures. As Archie trotted along behind Emily and Mr. Thornton, Emily couldn't help but grow excited at the prospect of exploring the place with her friend.

As if reading her mind, Mr. Thornton looked down at her, his mustache wiggling as he spoke. "Emily, this is your home now. I want you to feel welcome here."

At his words, a light giggle tickled Emily's ear, like the buzzing of a bee or a fly. She glanced around her shoulder, expecting to see something or someone . . . but there was nothing.

Mr. Thornton had stopped when she had, and he looked down at her with a small frown. "What's wrong?" he asked her, dark brows pulled together to shadow his eyes.

"Did you hear that?" Emily asked, unsure.

Mr. Thornton's frown deepened. "Hear what?"

"Um . . ." Emily shook her head. "Nothing."

The two continued on down the hall, stopping in front of a simple-looking door with a brass lock and handle. "I hope you like your new room." Mr. Thornton then pulled out a large brass key ring from his pocket, his long fingers moving through the fifty-some-odd keys until he found the one he was looking for. Mr. Thornton slid it inside the lock and, following a satisfying click, pushed the door open and gestured for Emily to enter.

Holding her breath (though she wasn't sure why), Emily stepped into the room, Archie at her side.

Her room was simply perfect.

The furniture was made of a deep cherrywood with white lace doilies decorating the surfaces of the armoire, dresser, and vanity. The canopy bed was tidy, its white sheets neatly tucked, with lavender accents on the pillows and dust ruffles. The rug near the fireplace had a design with light, pale colors that stood out against the dark wood floor.

Archie immediately claimed the rug, curling up in its center and resting his head on his paws. His eyes closed at once, and Emily resisted the urge to pat his head. He must have been exhausted after a frightening carriage ride and a stressful bath.

Mr. Thornton waited patiently at the threshold of the door while Emily explored the room, her fingers stroking the waxed wood and the fluffy sheets.

"Is this really all mine?" Emily wondered out loud, more to herself than asking Mr. Thornton, as she opened the armoire to find a row of neat cream-and-lace nightgowns.

"Of course this is all yours. This is your home now. We want you to be comfortable, and . . ."

Emily turned back to Mr. Thornton. He was watching her with a careful, guarded expression. Then he reached into his pocket and withdrew his brass key ring. It jangled and clinked with all the keys falling neatly against one another. He held it out and placed it into her outstretched hands.

"Feel free to explore as you wish. These keys are yours now."

Emily ran her fingers over the cool jagged metal and felt her excitement mount. She'd just been given a set of keys to her new castle. She could go anywhere she wished! She could spend days and days exploring the manor and learning all its secrets.

Maybe by learning its secrets, Blackthorn Manor would feel less creepy and mysterious to her. It would begin to feel more like a home.

"However"—Mr. Thornton knelt down, coming to her at eye level and wagging one finger in front of her nose—"there is one room, directly above yours"—he pointed to the ceiling—"that you must *never* go into."

"Why not?" Emily asked before she could stop herself.

Mr. Thornton placed a gentle but firm hand on her head and ruffled her dark hair. "It is a private place to your mother and me, and I ask you to respect this. Can you do that?"

At the words *your mother and me*, Emily's face flushed with warm pleasure and she knew, without a doubt, that this was a dream come true. She had parents who had given her a beautiful room, accepted her best friend, and allowed her an entire castle to explore. What was one off-limits room out of so many open to her? What was one rule compared to an endless list of them at Evanshire's?

Besides, she desperately wanted to please her new father.

Vigorously, she nodded her head and said, "Yes, P-Papa."

Mr. Thornton smiled beneath his mustache and patted her head. "Good girl. Now, have a pleasant sleep."

With that, he left her with the ring of keys and Archie

sleeping soundly on the rug. As soon as the door closed with a click, her gaze drifted to the ceiling. She promised herself that she'd never betray the trust of her new parents by venturing to the west wing on the third floor.

Even so, her mind couldn't help but wander . . .

# 5

The sunlight that escaped through the window curtains and snuck inside the cracks of the canopy bed teased Emily's eyelids. She blinked, dazed, forgetting where she was. For a frightening moment, she expected to see Miss Evanshire's face hovering over hers, screaming at her for sleeping late and missing chores, threatening no supper for a week.

Her heart rate calmed when she remembered what had happened the day before. As if to reinforce that this moment wasn't still a pleasant dream, Archie poked his head through her curtains and licked her fingers.

"Good morning, boy," she said with a smile, scratching behind his ears.

For a few moments, she allowed herself to enjoy the sunlight and the simple fact that she didn't have to be out of bed, splashing her face with frigid water, and then immediately cleaning every inch of the upstairs floor.

Finally, when her stomach prodded at her for nourishment, Emily hopped out of bed, but she shivered at the freezing floor against her bare feet. In fact, the entire room felt deathly cold—almost as cold as a room would be in the winter, not in the early summer. After changing out of one of the nightgowns that had been in the armoire and back into her old smock—the only day dress she had—Emily tugged on her worn shoes to protect her bare feet from the icy floor. Fully dressed, she went to her new vanity, trying to comb her bedhead hair that seemed to stick out in every direction.

As she reached for a ribbon in the drawer to tie back her dark locks, a pitter-patter of noise came from above.

Emily paused, frowning up at the ceiling. Were those

footsteps she heard? It was too distant and too muffled to tell. More likely, it was just mice scampering between the walls, but she shivered anyway. The room really was too cold.

Maybe she could ask Mr. Thornton for a fire before she went to bed tonight.

She was just tying the ribbon into her hair when a knock startled her. Archie gave a worried bark, and Emily shushed him with a finger to her lips. "Hush, boy."

Before she'd even reached the door, it swung open with Miss Greer standing at the threshold, a basket of laundry balancing on her hip.

"Planning to sleep away the day, Miss Emily?" she asked, an eyebrow raised, but with a smile to indicate her teasing.

Emily blushed. "I guess I was tired. Can I help you, Miss Greer?"

The older housekeeper waved the offer away. "No, no, I'm fine. Come, breakfast is ready for you. If you wait much longer, it will be teatime!"

At that, Miss Greer headed down the hallway, and Emily hurried after her, Archie following dutifully behind.

Down at breakfast, once more having her meal in the scullery, Emily helped herself to only a small portion from the spread that Miss Greer had laid out before her. When the old maid saw the meager helping, she shoveled Emily's plate high with bread and sausage while fussing under her breath, "Not nearly enough meat on your bones, miss. A walking skeleton, you are!"

Emily didn't dare argue and ate quietly and quickly, occasionally sliding bits of sausage under the table. Archie's tongue tickling her fingers alerted her that the sausage was greatly appreciated.

"Where are Mr. and Mrs. Thornton—I mean, Mama and Papa?" Emily finally asked, after swallowing a particularly rich bite of bread and butter.

"They headed off to London early this morning to do some shopping," Miss Greer said as she stirred the pot on the stove. It smelled like stew—maybe it was for the midday meal or evening supper. "They wanted to take you, but Mrs. Thornton worried you would be far too tired for another journey to London so soon after you arrived. She turned out right because you slept quite late."

Emily blushed again. While she was sorry to have missed her new parents, she was glad not to have to ride for hours in a carriage again. Plus, she was very eager to explore Blackthorn Manor.

Emily took a sip of her tea. "What are they shopping for?"

"They wanted to buy you a few nice dresses for your new wardrobe. You can't continue wearing that old smock," Miss Greer said, gesturing with her spoon toward Emily's ratty orphanage dress.

An excited thrill flushed Emily's cheeks deeper at the idea of a pretty new dress, and she had to stuff her mouth with another sausage to stop herself from asking more questions. She didn't want Miss Greer to think her too nosy.

"So what are you up to today, Miss Emily?" Miss Greer

turned back to her pot and added some kind of herb to the concoction.

The brass key ring seemed to grow heavy in Emily's dress pocket, as if it knew how deeply Emily desired to use it.

She shrugged. "I thought I'd look around a little."

"Well, that sounds fun," Miss Greer said, sticking her head into the pot, then wrinkling her nose and adding another handful of herbs. "If you decide to go outside, stay close. Always be within sight of the manor. You don't want to get lost and have Mr. Thornton go search for you."

"No, ma'am," Emily agreed. She pushed away her breakfast and tucked her hands under her thighs, wondering how long she had to wait before she could be dismissed to start her adventure.

A few minutes passed before Miss Greer glanced over her shoulder and her eyebrows flew up into her gray curls. "You're still here? Go on, then, child!"

Emily launched herself from the scullery table, Archie's nails clicking on the stone floor as he raced after her.

She hardly knew where to begin. If Blackthorn Manor

was her very own castle full of secrets, then how could she uncover them?

Halting in front of the grand staircase leading up to the second floor, she ignored all the shadows and cobwebs and imagined that it could be used for balls where princesses and princes would make their big entrance, arm-in-arm, wearing silk and velvet.

She looked to her left and right. Besides the entrance hall and the scullery, she had no idea what rooms were on the first floor. What sort of rooms were they?

Well, she had to start somewhere, but before she could pick a direction, Archie bounded up the steps. Surprised, but somewhat excited, Emily followed. Her feet padded against the carpet, past the second floor, and up the final set to the third floor.

Like most pointers, Archie followed his nose and his natural-born hunter instincts. Where they led him to, Emily had no idea but was eager to find out. He darted to the left, and as Emily took a few steps she realized exactly where Archie seemed to be headed.

The room right above hers—Mr. and Mrs. Thornton's forbidden room.

"Whoa, boy," she said, grabbing Archie gently around the neck. The dog whined, but Emily didn't let go.

The truth was, now that she was closer to the room, her curiosity had become ten times stronger. Emily was sure that if she ventured farther down the hall, that desire to disobey would only increase. And she *wouldn't* betray her new parents' trust, especially on only her second day.

Better to remove the temptation at all. So she turned them both around to head down the steps.

Back on the first floor, Emily set off down the eastern wing this time, Archie sniffing along beside her.

As she turned down the hallway, Emily smothered a scream with her hands.

Her cry came out high and muffled as she pressed her fingers against her lips, while her horrified gaze lingered on a great red deer positioned against the wall. Its lifeless eyes stared down at her, antlers sharp as fire pokers and muscles strong and pronounced underneath the light red-brown fur.

Even Archie growled next to her, hackles raised, and Emily had to put a hand on his head to calm him. The buck was obviously quite dead, but that was somehow worse than a live deer in a house. The way it just stood there frozen, watching her with black eyes, made her skin crawl.

Quickly, Emily moved past the deer, anxious to get as far as possible from it. Maybe, when she'd been here a year or so, she could ask Mr. Thornton to move the creature elsewhere, in a room she'd never have to visit again.

The first door Emily used her key ring on looked ordinary enough. It was so ordinary that it took Emily five tries until she found the right key to unlock it. She stepped inside, leaving the door cracked behind her. Immediately, Archie started poking his nose into the corners and legs of the furniture while Emily stood there, taking in the decor.

It was a study of some sort with a two-person sofa, a chintz armchair, a fireplace, and a desk. It was hard to tell the color of the furniture because everything in the room was coated in a thick layer of dust. Emily worried that if she breathed too hard or sneezed, she'd be caught in a heavy dust storm. To confirm her theory, she ran her finger across the surface of the desk, leaving behind a clear mark. The bright cherrywood shone underneath so rich and red that Emily thought it a great pity the desk was buried underneath the layer of gray.

Next to the desk was a floor-to-ceiling bookshelf built into the wall, holding all sorts of things like old maps, big leather-bound books, and a globe. She reached up to touch the latter, when a big black thing scurried across the sepia-toned sphere.

Emily yelped, jumping back with a disgusted shudder. She hated spiders!

The creature, with its long black legs crawling unnaturally, emerged on the globe's handle and moved across to its glittering silver web attached to the deep corner of the bookshelf. Emily turned away, not wanting to see any more of the spider or its web.

She distracted herself by inspecting a couple of sea paintings above the sofa. As she admired the artist's brushstrokes depicting sea spray clashing against rocks, the temperature in the room seemed to drop. It reminded Emily of her room that morning, except this wasn't left over from the late-night chill. Rather, it seemed to get colder by the second. Soon, goose bumps decorated her arms and her hair stood on end, while her teeth chattered.

*How did it get so cold?*

Emily was about to open her mouth to call for Archie when she heard a tiny squeaking noise. Confused, she turned in a circle, looking for the source of the sound. Her feet and her heart stopped when she saw the door slowly inching closed on its own.

The creaking grew louder as the big, heavy door strained on its hinges.

It was a creepy sight, but Emily urged her nerves to calm down. Doors did that all the time at the orphanage. There would be a cold draft, and then the door would swing shut loudly, frightening all the girls. Nothing to worry about. But still, she dearly hoped all the rooms weren't like this.

Unfortunately, the next two were.

One was a small bedroom with a bed and a big quilt of flowers that had probably once been full of vibrant colors but were now faded with age. In this room, too, dust covered all the furniture, and the mirror that sat on the armoire was rusting on the edges and cracked, distorting Emily's reflection. In the briefest of moments, Emily could've sworn she saw something in the corner of the mirror, but the cracks made it hard to tell what was real and what wasn't.

There was a big window with thin curtains, holes dotting the hem—probably the result of moths. Driven away by the thought of more insects, Emily ventured into the next room.

This one was also a bedroom, except instead of just dust, it smelled strongly of mildew. A large water spot stretched from one corner of the ceiling outward. It looked like it had long since dried, but the water had done its damage on the wood, leaving the room with a bad case of mold.

Leaving the bedroom and its smells behind, Emily made her way down the halls, wondering which door she should try next. As her dress kicked around her shins, Archie began to playfully nip at her heels, and before long the two were running down the halls, chasing each other. Her laugh bounced off the walls as Archie's tail slipped through her fingers, and he ran a few paces ahead, turning and throwing his paws forward, his tail wagging high in the air. That's when Emily realized something that sent a chill down her spine:

She wasn't the only one laughing.

Emily froze, the laugh dying in her throat. But the other giggle—the airy, light giggle that somehow reminded her of Mrs. Thornton—still drifted down the hallway from behind.

Archie stopped, too. His head cocked to the side as if he was listening intently to the laugh as well.

Too spooked to turn around, Emily ran down the hall, passing the scary buck, rounding the bend, and running into a solid stomach and pair of legs under a stained apron.

Emily looked up to find Miss Greer staring down at her

with her hands on her hips. "What on God's green earth are you doing, child?"

Breathless, Emily cast a look behind her shoulder. Of course there was nothing. She felt Archie nudge her waist and she swallowed, drawing strength from his presence.

"Nothing, I was just . . ." She paused a moment to catch her breath, then continued, "Exploring with Archie."

"Really? And what did you find that was so funny?"

Mouth open, Emily slowly shook her head, not sure how to respond, her thoughts still on the laughter that had come from behind her.

"Well?"

Miss Greer eyed her, and Emily knew she had to say something normal so the housekeeper would begin to accept her as part of the Thornton family, but instead, Emily blurted, "I heard someone laughing."

"Yes, that was you," Miss Greer said impatiently, taking Emily's shoulders and steering her down the hall.

"No—it wasn't—"

"My dear, I have much to do. Why don't you try

exploring outside? There are some lovely blackberry bushes you could pick from. If you pick me a bucketful, I might make a pie."

Emily didn't mind in the least that Miss Greer was so obviously trying to get rid of her. She nodded and headed for the scullery with Archie right behind.

After fetching a bucket and emerging into the sunshine, Emily felt her nervousness begin to dissipate. She was already excited at the prospect of picking blackberries, which she'd never done before. In fact, the one time she'd even tasted a blackberry had been during a rare dessert the girls had received on Easter Sunday. She honestly didn't think she'd ever have one again. Yet here they were, bushes of them.

The sight of the plump blackberries hanging heavily on their brambles made Emily's mouth start to water. Before she took another step, though, a furry little creature—a rabbit, most likely—darted under the brambles and Archie took off after it.

"Archie, no!" she called, but it was far too late. Archie

was gone in the bushes as fast as his prey. "Leave him alone, boy!" she cried, running around the bushes.

But she did not find Archie behind the blackberries. She found . . . another girl.

In fact, Emily almost ran into her, making the girl drop her apron, along with all the blackberries she'd been collecting. The girl looked to be about Emily's age, with blond curls and bright blue eyes—a very different sight from Emily, to be sure.

"I'm sorry! I didn't mean to startle you." Emily crouched down to gather the berries. "I wasn't really expecting to see anyone else here."

There was a rustling of skirts, and then the girl joined Emily on the ground, her dress tucked under her knees. "You're also a surprise. I wasn't expecting you, either."

Emily glanced up, her eyes catching on a glimmer of gold around the girl's neck. It was a lovely golden heart-shaped locket. Emily was so close that she could even read the inscription: *KAT.*

"Kat," Emily said, without thinking, "is that your

name?" Emily's gaze lifted from the locket to the girl's face.

The girl was smiling, but it didn't seem to touch her bright blue eyes. She shrugged and picked up another blackberry.

"Do you live around here?" Emily asked.

She shrugged again. "You could say that."

"Oh, well, I'm Emily." Thinking Kat a bit strange, Emily dropped the recovered blackberries into the girl's lap. "It was nice to meet you."

She started to get up when Kat grabbed Emily's dress and tugged her back down. "Don't leave so soon. We can pick blackberries together." This time, when Kat smiled, the grin lit up her face. "I can show you all the best spots."

A little thrill went through Emily at not only the idea of finding the best blackberry patches, but also the possibility of a new friend. Though she loved Archie with all her heart, it would be nice to have a companion that would actually talk back.

"Lead the way!" Emily said, returning the smile.

Still grinning, Kat beckoned Emily deeper into the bushes, weaving under the bigger brambles and avoiding the harsh thorns. Sure enough, they emerged into a little clearing surrounded by the lushest blackberries Emily had ever seen. Even without having any frame of reference, she knew they were impressive.

Immediately, Emily plucked a berry and popped it into her mouth. The juice was sweet and sour and delicious. Emily had always loved strawberries, but maybe she'd found a new favorite fruit.

"How did you find these bushes?" Emily asked.

Kat shrugged. "I spend a lot of time around here." Her voice was tinged in sadness, maybe even a little wistful. "So I know all Blackthorn's good places—inside and outside, like the back of my hand."

Immediately Emily thought of the laugh—the laugh that had scared her so much. Could that have been Kat? But before she had a chance to ask, Kat turned to Emily with a fierce gaze, her blue eyes so sharp they almost seemed to burn. "What about *you?*"

"What about me?" Emily asked, confused.

"I've never seen you before. Why did *you* come here?"

"Mr. and Mrs. Thornton—they adopted me," Emily said, feeling a little small under Kat's withering gaze.

Kat's eyes narrowed further, but she said nothing in response.

"What about you?"

"What about me?" Kat asked, echoing Emily's reply.

"Where is your family?"

This earned Emily a deep scowl from Kat, her face pale with anger. "My family doesn't care about me. They haven't for quite some time. I don't like talking about them."

Kat's words were so cold and waspish that Emily almost winced. "All—all right" was the only thing Emily could say.

How strange. What did Kat mean by that? How could her family no longer care about her? Was she an orphan, too?

Then Kat's expression softened a little. "I'm sorry. Don't worry about me. Technically I'm not supposed to be here, so you won't tell anyone on me, will you?" Kat held a finger to her lips and gave Emily an imploring look.

Emily thought of her time at Evanshire's Home for Neglected Girls and understood Kat's feeling of pain and rebellion, probably better than most girls would. Sneaking out to see Archie and finding new ways to keep him hidden, while nerve-racking, was still a bit exciting. And she had relished those small victories. They made her feel less trapped, the world less hopeless.

Emily nodded. "I promise."

With Kat's help, the blackberry picking was a wild success. In no time at all they had filled the bucket for Miss Greer, and Emily could almost taste the promised blackberry pie.

As they neared the doors to the manor, Emily turned to Kat, suddenly feeling a little embarrassed to ask her what she wanted. But it didn't matter. Kat beat her to it.

"Emily, would you like to play again tomorrow?"

Emily's grin was huge as a feeling of warmth spread through her chest all the way to her toes. "I'd love that."

Kat gave her a tiny, mischievous smile, then turned and ran back from where she came, her blond curls bouncing off her shoulders.

As her new friend left, Emily squeezed the handle of her heavy bucket and whistled through her teeth for her old friend.

That night marked Emily's first official meal with her new family. As they sat in the fancy dining room with the elegant chandelier and ornate silverware, Emily couldn't help but feel woefully unprepared and out of place. She preferred the scullery, with its warm fire, comforting scents, and the noise of clanging pots and pans as Miss Greer bustled about.

But at the same time, she was excited to be finally eating with her new parents.

As it turned out, a day shopping in London was exactly what Mrs. Thornton had needed. She was brighter and cheerier than before, gushing animatedly about the dresses she had found for Emily.

"Oh, Emily dear, you will *adore* this lavender dress I found. It will be such a nice contrast to your lovely dark hair."

Emily flushed with pleasure. Never had her hair been called *lovely* before.

Mr. Thornton, too, was good-natured, though not quite as talkative as Mrs. Thornton. He nodded and smiled when appropriate.

Finally, Mrs. Thornton fixed Emily with a steady gaze. "And what did you do today, darling?"

"I met—" Emily stopped abruptly, remembering her promise to Kat to keep her a secret.

"You what, dear?" Mrs. Thornton encouraged, lifting a spoonful of stew to her lips.

"I . . . went blackberry picking and picked enough for a pie," Emily finished.

But apparently that had been the wrong thing to say as well, because at Emily's words, Mrs. Thornton's face fell in a mask of devastation. She dropped her cutlery involuntarily, the resulting clatter echoing through the hall, then leaned back in her chair, her hand over her eyes.

Mr. Thornton and Emily exchanged worried looks. "Are you quite well, Charlotte?" Mr. Thornton asked.

"I . . ." Mrs. Thornton began softly. "I think I will turn in early."

Before Emily could say another word, her new mother was gone from the table in a rustle of blue silk skirts. Mr. Thornton stood to go after his wife, but then turned to Emily, his face severe and somewhat . . . sad. "No more blackberry picking. Are we clear, Emily?"

"Y-yes, sir." Emily was so startled she forgot to mention that it had been Miss Greer who suggested it in the first place.

Now she was left alone at the long table, not knowing what else to do, or what, exactly, she had done wrong.

After Emily helped Miss Greer clear the table, she left the dining room, still confused. As she recalled the events of the day in her mind, trying to make some sense of what had happened, she found herself suddenly in an unfamiliar hallway. It looked different than any other part of the manor she'd seen so far: The moldings were fresh and pristine, while the cobwebs and the dust were gone. It was as if the hallway was new, as if Emily had gone back in time to when the manor was first built, back to its original majesty.

She kept on walking. And walking. She walked for so long that her feet began to ache. But she didn't stop. Every step she took brought her closer to the room at the end of the hall.

The forbidden room.

But why? What was in there?

Emily kept walking.

When she thought about stopping, a voice whispered near her ear, *"You're almost there."*

And Emily would walk faster.

Soon, she was running. She felt the need to run like something behind her was chasing her, and the room at the end of the hall was her only escape.

She was too scared to look over her shoulder. She didn't want to see *what* was chasing her. A monster? A demon? Spring-Heeled Jack?

Whatever was after her was silent as a shadow.

No matter how far Emily ran, the door never got closer. It was too far away for her even to tell what it looked like, but Emily kept running, her lungs screaming at her to stop. But she had to go or that something would catch her, grab her, and devour her, or whatever it was that monsters did.

As a cold breath tickled her neck, Emily ran faster, and the door seemed to stop, allowing her to catch up, as she felt someone—or something—brush against her shoulder. Suddenly, the door slowly creaked open, revealing just the tiniest sliver of light . . .

But her arm was too short. She couldn't reach. An icy grip tightened on her arm and wrenched her back, back . . .

Emily woke with a wail. Floundering in her bed and fluffy pillows, she ripped herself out of the sheets and tumbled to the floor, Archie greeting her with a dozen licks to her face.

Wrapping her arms around the neck of her friend, she breathed in his familiar scent as she repeated to herself, "Just a dream. Just a dream. Just a . . ."

But that hadn't been a dream; it was a nightmare. Maybe the worst she'd ever had. She couldn't remember anything so frightening in her life. She *still* felt like running away as far as she could.

Even if it was a nightmare, though, it still wasn't real.

It must have been because of her terrible curiosity the day before. When she and Archie had almost gone down the third-floor west wing toward the door. Her mind didn't want to let it go.

*Well, you'll just have to,* Emily told herself.

Picking herself up off the floor, she straightened her sheets and put on one of the dresses that Mrs. Thornton had mentioned at supper the night before.

It was a lovely lavender dress that stopped below her knees with a lavender ribbon Emily used to tie back her dark hair. She couldn't help hoping that her choice in this dress would make Mrs. Thornton forgive her for whatever she'd done or said wrong last night.

Or maybe it hadn't been her fault at all.

But she couldn't help suspecting it had been the blackberry picking because of Mr. Thornton's reaction. Did Mrs. Thornton not like blackberries? Did she have a bad reaction to them?

Regardless, Emily hoped the dress would please her new mother in *some* way—that is, if Emily even ended up seeing her at all that day. Once again, Emily found herself in the scullery for breakfast, eating alone except for Archie curled under the table, and Miss Greer off doing laundry. Emily was just finishing her bowl of porridge when she heard a familiar giggle coming from behind her.

Invisible fingers seemed to brush her neck and send shivers down her spine at the laughter. Still remembering the nightmare, Emily twisted around, preparing to scream at whatever it was that had followed her into the waking world. She breathed a heavy sigh of relief when she saw Kat standing in the doorway, pressed against its frame, smiling.

"You scared me!" Emily said. She hadn't heard any door open at all. "How did you get in?"

Kat held her finger up to her lips in the same mischievous way she had yesterday and smiled. "I told you, I know everything about this place."

As Kat took a step closer to Emily, Archie emerged from under the table, where he had been waiting for Emily to drop some scraps, a growl rumbling in his throat.

Emily put her hand on the top of his head, surprised to find her usually friendly dog acting so territorial. "It's all right, boy. Kat's a friend, too."

Kat narrowed her eyes at the dog and Archie's ears pulled back, but his growling had stopped.

"He can't understand you, Emily. He's a dog. Now let's go play." Kat turned on her heel and hurried around the corner, her skirts and blond curls whipping out of view.

But Archie was more than just a dog to Emily, and she was quite sure that he did understand her. At least most of the time. She rubbed the top of his head affectionately. "You coming, boy?"

"Emily!" Kat called.

Not wanting to lose or irritate Kat, Emily left Archie, but the sound of paws against the wood floor told her that he was right behind her like always.

Kat led Emily and Archie up to the third floor, east wing, down the hall and around a corner into a small room that was so plain and unnoticeable, Emily was sure that she would have overlooked it had she been exploring on her own.

It had some old dusty furniture tucked into a corner, half-draped in plain white sheets, but other than that, the room was bare. What were they doing in here?

Emily was about to ask Kat that very question, but stopped at the sight of the girl crouching in the opposite corner of the room. Stepping up behind her just in time to see Kat slide open a hidden door in the wall, Emily's mouth popped open in astonishment.

"How . . . how did you know it was there?" Emily practically stuttered. "Where does it lead to?"

"You'll have to come along if you want to find out," Kat called over her shoulder as she stepped fearlessly through the secret sliding panel.

Emily tugged at her bottom lip with her teeth, glancing around the small room. Surely Mr. and Mrs. Thornton wouldn't get mad about her exploring unknown places—apart from the forbidden room, of course. Besides, they probably wouldn't find out anyway, unless she elected to tell them. The manor was so big, it was unlikely anyone would hear anything at all.

Her decision made, Emily hunched over and stepped through the hidden door, following Kat into a world even dustier than the one they'd left. And that was saying something.

A whine came from behind her. Emily looked over her shoulder to find Archie hovering at the secret passageway's entrance. His feet danced lightly up and down, and he paced. Clearly, he was torn between his fear of going through the small space and his desire to follow Emily.

"Stay there, boy," she called. "I'll be back!" Then she turned to focus on her new surroundings.

Despite the dust, Emily couldn't help but feel awestruck. The manor's roof was constructed at a slant, and the windows were built on the sides way above their heads so the morning sun rained down in distinct sections, separated by shadows. Dust motes floated in the air, and the wind whistled through the windows. Except for the creak of the floorboards from Emily's footsteps and the pounding of her heart, everything was silent. Not even a mouse scampering was heard.

She kept her gaze trained on Kat's back, trying to step where she stepped and hoping that they would get where they were going soon.

"How much farther?" Emily couldn't stop herself from asking.

"Not much," Kat answered without looking back.

A few minutes later, Kat came to a small crawl space. In many ways, it was like a tunnel made of old wood and cobwebs, but the slanted wood boards overhead didn't completely connect, so the air flowed freely. It didn't make Emily feel any better about the situation, though. She thought of the spider crawling across the globe and took a step back.

Without any hesitation, Kat got down on her hands and knees and began crawling, her petite form easily going under the wood, her blond hair not even brushing the cobwebs.

From inside the crawl space, Kat beckoned Emily with a large grin. "C'mon, scaredy-cat."

Emily clenched her jaw and dropped down on her hands and knees, trying to ignore how much bigger and broader she was compared to Kat. She would still be able to fit . . . right?

Oh so carefully, Emily made her way through, her breath stalled tight in her lungs. Her shoulders brushed against the wood, and the fragile cobwebs broke at the lightest touches of her dress and hair. But, thankfully, she fit.

She was just about to breathe out a sigh of relief as she emerged from under the wood when she heard a loud noise.

*RIIIP.*

Heart dropping to her stomach, Emily whirled around to find a terribly long tear in her new lavender dress. A piece of it was still snagged on the old wood. Dismayed, Emily desperately ran her fingers over the fabric, feeling how large it was. There was no way it could be hidden.

She didn't even want to picture how devastated Mrs. Thornton would be.

Unbidden, tears sprang to her eyes and she sniffed, trying to shove it down. How could she be so careless to ruin her new dress—a gift from her parents?

Next to her, Kat smothered a giggle, and Emily glared at her.

"It's not my fault," Kat declared haughtily. "You should

be more careful. Now come on, don't you want to see where we end up?"

To be honest, Emily didn't much care anymore, but they'd already come this far. She felt she had to see it through.

As it turned out, the secret entrance led to a music room. Like the rest of the mansion, it was in a sore state. But because the large harp and grand piano were covered in sheets, Emily couldn't help but marvel at how perfectly maintained they were when she uncovered them.

Kat hopped up on the piano bench and immediately began to play a few notes. She wasn't very good, but Emily could tell she'd had at least a few lessons. The tune was light and quick, an easy melody to remember and get stuck in your head.

"Do you want me to teach it to you?" Kat asked, sliding over and patting the spot on the bench beside her.

Emily had always wanted to learn how to play an instrument. Given the choice, she would have preferred a violin, but learning on a grand piano sounded equally exciting, so she slid on the bench next to Kat and watched the girl as she once again played the melody.

Kat was surprisingly patient as she taught Emily's fingers to move in a pattern over the keys. She had just finished showing Emily one sequence when she suddenly froze and jumped off the bench, hurrying off toward the secret door.

Emily was just about to call after her but then heard pounding, hurried footsteps down the hall. In seconds, Miss Greer was there, red-faced and out of breath.

"Heavens! Miss Emily! What do you think you're doing?"

Emily glanced behind her, but Kat had disappeared. Goodness, she was fast!

"I . . . I was just playing on the piano," Emily said, gesturing to the piano before her.

Miss Greer pulled Emily off the bench, placed the lid over the keys, and grabbed the sheet off the floor, draping it over the beautiful instrument. "Well, none of that, you hear? It's a miracle Mrs. Thornton didn't hear you. It would upset her deeply."

"Does she not like music?" Emily asked, simultaneously wondering why they would have a piano at all, in that case.

"It's not that, it's . . ." Miss Greer stopped, frowning severely. "Never you mind. Just go freshen up, it's about teatime and— My word! What happened to your new dress?" she exclaimed, pointing to the large rip in the lavender fabric.

Emily's face and neck flushed with heat. "It was an accident," she mumbled, scuffing her shoe into the carpet.

"Well, I should hope you wouldn't do that on purpose," Miss Greer sighed. "It's fine, dear. Just lay it out tonight and I'll find time to repair it."

Emily looked up at her, too embarrassed and guilty to look hopeful or relieved. "Really?"

"Yes, dear. Just be more careful next time." Miss Greer patted Emily's head. "And no more piano."

Emily nodded, but she couldn't help but begin to keep a running tally of all the things that were now forbidden: the mysterious room, blackberries, and music. Still, she shouldn't complain. Blackthorn Manor was a palace compared to Evanshire's. She just hated to keep upsetting her new family.

She would stay in and read a book tomorrow. Surely she couldn't get in trouble with that.

The next morning she had breakfast with Mr. Thornton in the fancy dining room, but Emily was almost too nervous to eat anything of real substance. She nibbled on some dry toast and porridge, unable to remember anything but Mr. Thornton's stern look from the night she'd mentioned the blackberries.

Of course, there was something else on her mind that morning as well. She'd heard some strange noises above her head last night and just knew that they were coming from the forbidden room above her bedroom. It had taken her so long to fall asleep that she had even considered going into the Thorntons' room to tell them.

In the end she had fallen asleep, but she lit more candles than necessary to keep the encroaching darkness at bay.

Now she sat at breakfast, stirring her porridge but not really eating it, and thinking about the room directly above hers. Even if she wanted to disobey the Thorntons and go inside—which she did *not*—there was no way for her to go in. She didn't have the key. It would be best to just forget about it. There was nothing to be done.

But why couldn't she?

"Is Mrs. Thornton not coming down for breakfast, sir?" Miss Greer asked as she poured another splash of milk into Mr. Thornton's tea.

"No, I'm afraid Charlotte is still not feeling well," he replied.

Mrs. Thornton was in her bedroom, and it seemed that Mr. Thornton was very worried about her. He didn't say much to Emily the whole morning. In fact, the only time he really looked at her was when she timidly asked if it was all right if she be excused.

Blinking at her, as if just noticing she was there, Mr. Thornton gave her a small nod. "Yes, my dear. What will you be doing today?"

Hoping that reading a book wouldn't upset him, like blackberry picking had upset his wife, or playing the piano had upset Miss Greer, she answered, "I was going to read a book."

At this, Mr. Thornton straightened, his eyes suddenly growing bright with interest. "A book, you say? Which one?"

Emily shrugged. "I'm not sure yet. I don't know where to look for any."

"Well, come then," he said, spirits slightly brighter. "I'll take you to my study and we'll pick out a good one."

Abandoning his hardly touched breakfast, Mr. Thornton moved around the table, took Emily's hand, and together they climbed the staircase to the second floor and turned toward the east wing—a part Emily had not yet had the time to explore. Archie trotted along behind them, having been snoozing under Emily's chair during breakfast. She was grateful that Mr. Thornton seemed not to pay the dog any mind at all. She even noticed that when Archie had sneezed under her chair, her new father had simply blinked a few times, checked under the table, and smiled with what looked like a hint of affection.

Pausing at the simple-looking door closest to the staircase, Mr. Thornton pulled out his own ring of keys and inserted a smaller brass one into the lock. The door swung open to reveal a homey study in a much better state than the rest of the mansion. It was as if Miss Greer made sure to keep this room clean more than the rest.

*Probably because Mr. Thornton spends so much time in it*, Emily reasoned.

Mr. Thornton strode immediately to a bookshelf and scanned the leather-bound titles. "Ah, here we go. Try this one." He handed Emily a maroon book with a small, round gold emblem on the cover. She opened it to read *Alice's Adventures in Wonderland by Lewis Carroll* on the title page.

"Have you read it before?" Mr. Thornton asked.

Emily shook her head while already opening up the book to the first page. Miss Evanshire didn't let the girls read any fiction, or anything other than religious texts, for that matter.

*She really was a soulless old bat*, Emily thought bitterly.

"It's very good. I think you'll rather enjoy it. I was always trying to get her to read, but she . . ." Mr. Thornton stopped and frowned, rubbing his jaw, his eyes suddenly losing their light. "Well, anyway. Give it a go, Emily."

Emily nodded eagerly. "I will!" She turned to go with Archie, but Mr. Thornton placed a hand on her shoulder.

"You're welcome to read here, if you wish." He gestured to a large red chintz armchair.

Thrilled at being able to stay with him, Emily hopped up onto the chair while Archie curled at her feet. She began to read diligently, but every once in a while she would sneak peeks at her new father as he sat at his office desk, scribbling away with a fountain pen.

Emily reveled in the comfortable silence. In fact, she

realized that time was passing only when Miss Greer came in with the tea. And even though very little was said while Miss Greer poured the hot concoction, Emily received a few soft smiles from Mr. Thornton. They left her feeling warm inside—and it wasn't from the tea in her belly. She was sure of it.

On the outside however, she was *freezing*.

The cold chill had happened suddenly and without warning. The draft seemed to fall on her as swiftly as a blizzard in the dead of winter. Her hands curled around the book in her lap, and she tried to stop her teeth from chattering.

Hoping more of the tea would get her warm again, she picked up the cup and brought it to her lips. As she was lowering it back down, something suddenly shoved her elbow, splashing her hot tea everywhere—on the front of her dress, on the arms of her chair, and . . . on the lovely book Mr. Thornton had given to her.

"Emily!" Mr. Thornton cried as soon as he realized what had happened. He sprang from his desk and ran to his daughter's side. "Are you all right? Did the hot water burn you?"

But Emily didn't respond. Her hands were shaking, and her breath was frozen in her chest. Had . . . had something shoved her? Was she just that clumsy? Whatever had happened, it had absolutely ruined the book in her lap. Tears welled in her eyes. It was just like the rip in her dress all over again. Why was this happening to her? A few droplets trickled down her cheeks as fear, frustration, and disappointment warred inside her chest.

*"It's your fault,"* a voice whispered.

For a moment, Emily couldn't tell if the words had been inside her head or next to her ear. They were so harsh and angry and frightening that Emily sucked in a breath, making more tears splash onto the already ruined pages.

"I-I'm so sorry, P-Papa," Emily stuttered, though whether her teeth chattered because of the cold or fear that she had once again upset her new father, she didn't know. "I didn't mean to soil the book."

Swiftly, Mr. Thornton lifted the novel off her lap and tugged her off the chair.

"No need to worry, my girl." He ruffled her hair gently and took her hand. "Shall we go outside and have a little bit of fun? You coming, boy?"

To her surprise, Mr. Thornton patted Archie on the head and he led both of them out of his study, down the hall, and out into the bright afternoon sunlight, the warmth of the sun washing away the cold chill in Emily's bones.

# 9

It had been the happiest day Emily could ever remember having. She tried to think back to her days at Evanshire's Home for Neglected Girls to see if there was one that could compare, but she honestly couldn't think of any. Not that she tried very hard. The days before Blackthorn Manor and her new parents were like those from another lifetime, memories layered in bruises and dripping with tears.

Exhausted, but full and content from Miss Greer's supper of beef stew with dumplings, Emily crawled into bed after changing into a pale pink nightgown that

Mrs. Thornton—*Mama*, Emily corrected herself—had given her.

After *Papa* had taken Emily outside, they played fetch with Archie until it was late in the afternoon and Miss Greer had to come and call them in for supper. To both Emily's and her father's surprise and delight, Mrs. Thornton had joined them at supper and seemed to be in a much more chipper mood. She even went up to Emily's bedroom and spent the next hour going through all of Emily's new clothes. She hadn't noticed the lavender dress was missing, and Emily guessed it was because there were so many others to look at. It was then that Mrs. Thornton had picked out the pink nightgown and said that it looked nice with Emily's dark hair.

It was just a nightgown, but Emily loved putting it on and knowing that Mrs. Thornton had been thinking of her when she bought it.

A whine from the right side of her bed made Emily giggle and roll to the edge to lean down. She was greeted by a lick on her nose.

"Sorry, boy," she said, scratching behind Archie's ears, "you know you can't sleep up here. Miss Greer would have a fit if she found dog hair in the sheets." It made Emily laugh again to think of Miss Greer's round face going red and shaking the sheets over Emily's head as she launched into an already familiar complaint: "As if I don't have enough work to do already, Miss Emily! Now I must wash for the dog as well?"

A light *knock, knock* on the door interrupted her imagination. Emily shot up in bed. Was it Miss Greer? Or maybe, dare she believe it, her new mother come to tuck her in? She wasn't sure if real parents did that at her age, but she dearly hoped so.

She leaped out of her large bed and ran to the door, swinging it wide open for . . .

Kat?

An odd jump of nerves in her stomach made Emily flinch at the idea that Kat really did know this manor far too well for her own good. Breaking and entering was a crime, wasn't it?

*Don't be silly, Emily! She's your friend.*

Kat stood in the threshold with a strangely cold expression on her face.

"Wh-what are you doing here?" Emily whispered, leaning out slightly to look up and down the hall. "Come in straightaway!"

While Emily had guessed that Kat's family didn't much care what she did with her time, considering she spent so much of it at the estate, she was still surprised to see her so late in the evening. But regardless of how Kat's family may or may not have felt about her being in the manor at such an hour, Emily was sure her own parents would not approve.

"I thought we could play a game of hide-and-seek," Kat said, her pale lips turning upward into a hint of a smile.

*No, more like a smirk*, Emily thought nervously. She'd seen that look before, when Agatha would swipe an extra piece of bread and then blame it on Emily.

"But . . ." Emily glanced back at her empty bed. "It's a little late. Maybe tomorrow morning?"

It was the wrong thing to say.

Kat stepped forward so fast, Emily could've sworn she felt a cold breeze tickle her skin. The girl narrowed her eyes at Emily, her lips twisting into a tight scowl. "I didn't get to play with you all day because you were *quite* busy." Her words were coated in anger, but Emily sensed a hint of hurt under them. "All I'm asking for is a quick game before bedtime. Am I your friend or not?"

"Of course you are. I just meant that . . ." Emily said, taking a tentative step backward, away from the intensity of Kat's gaze. "All right. I suppose one game wouldn't hurt."

Kat's scowl vanished, transforming into a pretty smile—the same smile that had drawn Emily to her in the first place.

"Don't worry, it won't be the whole house. That would take *ages.* I know just where to play. Follow me!" She threw her arm out in a big, expressive gesture and began skipping down the hall, her gold curls bouncing as she went.

Hesitating, but only for a moment, Emily turned back

inside her room and grabbed her key ring off the nightstand. "Come on, Archie," she said, clicking her tongue for her friend to follow. For a moment, she wondered if Archie would come, since he didn't seem to like the other girl much. But this time, the faithful canine was already by the door, as if he was waiting for her. Running her hand over his head, she hurried after Kat, and Archie trotted dutifully behind.

By the time Emily caught up to Kat, they were on the third floor. Kat had stopped at a door with a large brass handle and lock, bigger and grander than the doors to the other rooms Emily had encountered so far. Though, to be fair, she hadn't explored much of the third floor yet.

While Emily inspected the keys to decide which one to use, Kat tapped her foot impatiently, finally pointing to a large brass one in the middle of the ring. "It's that one."

Emily wasn't surprised to find that the key fit perfectly. She wasn't sure how, but Kat knew everything about Blackthorn—even the right keys to the right locks.

They entered the room and Emily let a gasp escape

her lips upon seeing stacks and stacks of beautiful leather-bound books. They were all kinds of colors and sizes. She couldn't believe that the Thorntons had such a collection. An entire library she could explore! She guessed Mr. Thornton kept his favorites in his study.

Feeling Kat watching her expectantly, Emily grinned in response. "Good idea."

Kat smiled again. This time the smile was halfway between a smirk and something genuine. Maybe Kat already had a hiding spot in mind.

Sure enough, Kat darted off into the stacks. "You're it!" she called over her shoulder.

Emily was fine with that, not that it would have mattered to the bossy Kat. It would give her time to look at all the different books. As Archie sniffed around the corners of the large bookcases, his overeager nose getting coated in dust and making him sneeze, Emily placed her hands over her eyes and counted aloud. Her voice echoed in the vast library.

"Ready or not, here I come!" Her words were met with

complete silence—a silence that sounded more hollow and ominous than before.

Emily shook the feeling off. It was the same as when she'd first started exploring the estate. Nothing but her imagination. Besides Archie, her imagination had been her only companion in the long lonely years at Evanshire's. It had to be that she just wasn't used to a big old house yet.

Yes, that *had* to be it.

Despite her logic, Emily found herself holding her breath as she moved through the rows of dusty, neglected books. They were big, tall things. Imposing, like so many other objects in this house. Shadows stretched across the floor and merged into one another, forming a blanket of darkness. The sun had long since dipped below the horizon, and the only light was from the full moon outside the window that night.

It really was that late.

*Just find Kat*, Emily thought to herself. But she was frustrated by the lack of distinct hiding places within the library. Why had Kat picked such a room?

No longer excited about seeing more of the library, Emily moved faster, her bare feet padding silently over the rug.

The lack of sound was disturbing. She hadn't noticed how quiet it had gotten, but now she felt like she couldn't even hear her own breathing. It was as if the shadows had sucked all the noise from the air, bringing it into their lair of darkness.

Then came the cold.

At first, Emily didn't notice much difference. She'd wandered out into the huge drafty house without her robe in only a nightgown and barefoot. Certainly she was bound to get a little chilly, but as the seconds ticked by, the temperature dropped. It dropped so much that when she moved her fingers they actually hurt, like her bones and muscles didn't want to cooperate in the frigid air.

It was like the cold in the study and in her bedroom. It felt physical and tangible. Unnatural.

Emily paused, listening for something. Anything. Where was Archie?

Another giggle issued from the looming darkness of the library. *"Down here,"* a voice called, beckoning her.

"Kat?" Emily responded, not knowing who else it would be.

Her pulse increasing, Emily moved on to the next row of shelves, then froze. Slowly, shadows began slithering down the volumes, moving like small hands. They seemed somehow alive, like they really *were* hands grabbing and clawing at the old leather books, dripping onto the pages and down their spines like spilt black ink.

Then a sudden memory came to her. Her first day at Blackthorn, Emily had seen shadows coming down the manor like this—alive and angry. Had that actually been real?

She felt something crawl over her own spine, as if the shadows had reached out to claim her as well.

Too scared to move or think, Emily didn't notice Archie's presence until he tugged at her nightgown with his teeth, growling furiously.

With a gasp, Emily finally found the strength to move, then stumbled out of the row of books before—

*CRASH.*

The bookshelf toppled onto the ground with a loud boom that shook the entire floor.

Emily fell to her knees and scrabbled backward against the wall, breathing wildly as Archie nuzzled his head into her lap. She could feel him shaking, too, his tail in between his legs.

Her pulse was skipping, heart pounding erratically in her chest like it couldn't decide if it wanted to start or stop.

Remembering the eerie feeling of fingers on her neck, Emily whimpered, pressing her shoulder blades harder against the wall. But no shadows moved around them. She could hear her breathing. She could move her fingers again.

*What happened?*

"What happened?" demanded a voice from above.

Emily nearly jumped out of her skin. She hadn't even seen Kat approach.

Kat looked down at her, hands on her hips, her expression concerned and annoyed at the same time.

"I . . . I . . ." Emily stammered. "The bookshelf . . ." She pointed a shaking finger at the overturned case, books scattered beneath it everywhere, old wood splintered to reveal pale, sharp edges of broken lumber.

Kat didn't bother looking over. She regarded Emily with a tilt of her head, and her big blue eyes looked almost silver in the moonlight. "You should be more careful."

"But I—"

"Shhh!" Kat hushed, then looked over her shoulder into the darkness. "I hear footsteps. Someone's coming."

"Maybe it's Miss Greer. She—"

"Remember what you promised me, Emily. You can't tell them I'm here or I'll get in trouble!" With that, Kat picked up her skirts and ran back through the library.

Emily wanted to call after her that she didn't want to be alone, not now, not after the living shadows and the bookshelf, but Kat was already gone. At least Archie stayed with her. Archie nuzzled her elbow as Emily got to her feet. The pup was as happy to have her as she was to have him.

Emily had barely moved before she heard footsteps—pounding ones—coming down the hall toward her.

Apparently Kat had been right.

Emily fought down a fresh wave of fear, hoping that it was someone she knew and not a monster or the puppet master of these creepy moving shadows.

No, that hadn't been real. There was no way it could've been real.

A deep male voice bellowed her name, getting closer and closer.

"Emily . . . Emily . . . Emily!"

*Mr. Thornton!*

Relief flooding through her, Emily raced to the door just in time to see both Thorntons and Miss Greer come in with panting breaths.

Trying to keep her voice from cracking, Emily told them what had happened, leaving out the part about Kat and their game. Kat's parting words echoed in her mind: *Remember what you promised me.*

Emily didn't mention the crawling shadows, either. It was her imagination, a nightmare. *It had to be. It just had to be.*

Mr. Thornton dropped down to one knee and took her shoulders. "As long as you're all right, my dear. But please, no more nighttime escapades."

Emily nodded, more than glad to oblige. "I promise," she said breathlessly. She was already adding the library to the increasing list of rooms she never wanted to enter again.

Emily stayed in bed until long after the sun filled her bedroom with golden light. After her new mother had tucked her in, Emily stayed awake for hours, watching the shadows dance beyond the small candle at her bedside. She was still afraid, worried that at any moment they could start slithering toward her like dark snakes.

But they didn't, and eventually she fell asleep to the sound of Archie's breathing and the occasional thump of his tail as he dreamed.

Now that it was morning, Emily wasn't sure if all

that she'd seen last night hadn't been any more than another nightmare. Perhaps she'd fallen asleep, or perhaps—

"Miss Emily, you'll sleep the day away!"

Miss Greer burst into the room like the sun herself, carrying a tray piled high with bread, butter, tea, sausage, a hard-boiled egg, and porridge with what smelled strongly of brown sugar.

Even though the fear still lingered in her gut, Emily's stomach won, growling eagerly in response to the sight and smell of such a full breakfast. Emily hurried around the bed, carefully stepping to avoid Archie, who was now lying on his back, basking in the warm sun on the rug.

"Thank you, Miss Greer," she said, taking the tray from the housekeeper.

"Mr. and Mrs. Thornton missed you at breakfast, my dear," she said, bustling around the room, picking up things to launder—things that Emily didn't even consider dirty—and bundling them into her large arms.

"I'm sorry, I didn't sleep very well."

"No, don't s'pose I would, either, after an incident like that. You stay away from those old bookshelves y'hear?" Miss Greer wagged a plump finger at her just as Emily was taking a large bite of bread and butter.

Emily hurried to swallow. "Yes, ma'am."

"Good. Don't need any more things breaking in this house. Why, just the other day, there . . ." Miss Greer trailed off, her usually rosy cheeks going just a little pale.

"What?" Emily asked, tensing slightly.

"Never you mind," Miss Greer called over her shoulder as she hurried for the door. "Stay out of the scullery, my dear. I've a lot of work to do."

After finishing her breakfast, Emily put on a simple blue cotton dress, patterned but not so fanciful that she would worry about getting it too dirty. She wanted to spend today outside. Yesterday, with her new father, had been so blissful that she thought maybe it was what she needed again—some hours spent in the sun where none of her fears or her imagination could get the best of her.

Archie was happy to join her. She raced him to the main staircase, her hand wrapping around the post and hanging on the ornate piece of wood as the dog danced around her waist, then pranced down the steps. Laughing, Emily took off after him through the hallways warmed with light from the open curtains, and out the side door Miss Greer used to enter and exit the manor. She preferred this door instead of the front ones—those were far too heavy.

Just as she'd remembered, the door led her out into an overgrown garden. It was full of life beyond anything that Emily could've imagined back at the orphanage. She'd thought the blackberry bushes where she'd first met Kat had been wild, but that was nothing. This was a magical place. It had the thick scent of honeysuckle in the air, thanks to the huge tangle of the stuff growing against the side of the manor. Weeds and flowers mingled together in one giant jungle. There were the bright orange petals of calendulas, the rich pink of the foxgloves, and the dusty purple of lavender. And though Emily didn't know very much about plants, she was able to tell which were the herbs because they were so well maintained, probably because Miss Greer used them in her cooking.

Emily was so caught up in the garden that she'd hardly noticed that Archie had begun to wander deeper into the weeds. She was just about to call him back when she felt a whisper of cold against her neck.

For a split second she was too scared to move, but then her reflexes caught up and she whirled around.

Kat stood less than a foot away, her hands tucked behind her back, an excited grin plastered on her face. "Found you."

Emily resisted the urge to scowl at her friend for scaring her. Had Kat blown on her neck? "We stopped playing that. And *I* was the one seeking, remember?"

"You don't have to get so mad. I told you why I had to leave," Kat huffed, folding her arms.

"I'm not mad," Emily replied, though she was slightly annoyed.

Before she could say anything else, Archie burst through the bushes next to them and skidded in front of Emily, beginning to bark ferociously at Kat.

Shocked, Emily pulled Archie by the collar as Kat backed away, her face tight with a little fear and a little anger. "Archie, no!" Emily had never heard Archie react that way to anyone before.

"What's wrong with that mutt?" Kat snapped.

"I don't know, he's never like this." Emily rubbed his muzzle in an effort to calm her friend. "Maybe he's just scared of what happened last night when we were together. You know, with the shadows." Quickly, she tried to explain to Kat what she'd seen, but the girl was shaking her head before she'd even finished.

"Emily, you know shadows can't move on their own," she grumbled. "You read too much."

"What does reading have to do with anything?"

Kat shrugged and looked to the right, then up, then

to the left, and back to Emily. "Never mind. I was going to show you the garden anyway. There's one place in particular you'll love. Come on." Kat beckoned Emily to follow, this time waiting at the edge of the path before stepping into the undergrowth of the overflowing plants.

Once again, Emily was amazed by all the places and hidden secrets of Blackthorn that Kat knew. The bookshelf had been a one-time occurrence, and she couldn't blame Kat for running away and not wanting to get into trouble. Emily's feet felt lighter at the prospect of learning even more about her new home.

With an encouraged grin, Emily followed Kat through the garden. Now much calmer, Archie trailed behind them, pausing to sniff almost everything, but trotting quickly to catch up if Emily got too far away. They passed hedges of laurel taller than their heads, and big patches of peonies and cowslips. Brambles caught at their stockings, but Kat didn't slow, not until they came to a well that was covered in moss and ivy so thick that Emily could barely see its stones.

Tiny daisies and clovers decorated the greenery over the well. Emily loved it very much. In her mind, it was a magical tunnel entrance to a world of fairies and Cornish pixies.

*If I looked over the edge, would I catch a glimmer of their light?*

"Come closer," Kat said, jumping between overly tall patches of flowers and weeds.

Emily did. She was transfixed by the mystical sight of the well and wanted to look over the side to see if what she was imagining was actually true. But a few steps away, she paused. She hated heights. If she looked down she'd probably just see darkness and a small hint of murky, muddy well water. Nothing to be excited about, or to scare herself over.

"You can't see into the well from all the way over there, silly," Kat said with a light, tinkling laugh.

*That laugh again.* Emily pushed the thought away as Archie whimpered at her side. She put a comforting hand on top of his head.

“I don’t need to see down. I’m fine here,” she said, running her suddenly sweaty hands over the front of her dress.

Kat’s expression slowly faded from a smile into something dark and angry. “Emily,” she said, her fists curling at her sides. “Come *here*.”

The command was so forceful Emily couldn’t help but comply. She didn’t want to face Kat’s anger. Hesitantly, she stepped up to the edge of the well and looked down. Besides the slight feeling of vertigo and disappointment that there were no fairy lights, Emily found that it was exactly as she expected: dark, with a trace of light shining on the stale, moldy water. Emily stepped back, but as she did, something caught her eye. On the edge of the well, the beautiful green moss and clovers started to turn brown and dead right in front of her eyes. Cold leeched off the stones like honey dripping from a beehive. Overhead, the sun that had warmed Emily’s cheeks, hands, and back suddenly vanished. It was quickly replaced by a chill that descended from above, not unlike the chill that overcame her in Mr. Thornton's study. Thick storm clouds, not uncommon on an English summer afternoon, transformed the entire garden into a world of gloom.

Despite the sudden and odd weather change, Emily couldn't tear herself away from staring down into the well. What she saw should have been impossible.

The decay grew rapidly, sweeping across the well's surface and sinking into the stones underneath. It was like her living shadows had moved from the manor to the garden to spread their dark disease. They seemed to be everywhere.

Emily gasped and tried to move her hands away from the well, but the cold held her in place, pulling her. Then the stones shifted—crumbling and falling down with a great splash. Losing her balance, Emily almost toppled after them into the well's sinister depths.

But Archie took hold of her dress by his teeth, growling and pulling. Teetering, Emily threw herself to the ground and took relief in the stability and solidness of the grass and earth under her.

Kat peered over her, eyes wide, gold hair hanging down in tendrils, and repeated her words from last night: "What happened?" Her face was hard to see, as she was backlit from the bright sunlight that had suddenly returned. Almost as if it had never left.

Heart pounding, Emily sat up and inched back, staring at the well. Half of its side had just crumbled away. Emily didn't know stones could do that. Had it been just like the bookcase? She felt as if she was going mad!

"I . . . I don't know," Emily said, trembling despite the fact that the air felt warmer and she could feel the sun on her face and arms again. Archie licked her cheek and she scratched his ears, still fighting off the feeling of almost falling.

Kat crouched down in front of her, soft blue eyes roaming over Emily as if checking for any obvious wounds. "It looks like part of the stones gave away. I'm glad you didn't fall in. That would've been *awful*."

"But it wasn't just the stones. The moss and grass

turned dead and—" Emily's explanation faded as Kat's brow furrowed deeper, obviously skeptical of the tale.

"Maybe you imagined it, Emily. Just like last night," Kat said, her tone calm and soothing. "Don't worry, there are other parts of the garden I can show you."

But all that hadn't been her imagination—it couldn't have been. It was right in front of her, after all. So the bookcase hadn't been her imagination, either. Although, she hadn't stayed around long enough to investigate the splintered wood and the squashed books.

Emily hated the idea of it, but felt like she had to go back and see for herself. Just in case.

They spent the rest of the late morning exploring the garden with no more strange incidents. Kat showed her all the different kinds of shrub roses and the small patch of strawberries that were constantly being nibbled on by rabbits. Thrilled at the possibility of seeing the furry little thieves, Emily made a mental note to return soon to the fruit patch.

At teatime, she heard Miss Greer calling for her from

the side door of the manor. She turned to invite Kat in for tea, but the girl had disappeared into the vast wilds of the garden.

It was just as well. Emily had decided to visit the library while it was still light out, and for some reason, she didn't want Kat with her when she did.

---

Archie sniffed the threshold of the library door. Emily held the key ring in her hand, but she was having a hard time preventing them from jangling. Her fingers just kept shaking.

What was she doing back here? What was she hoping to prove? That she wasn't imagining everything? That she wasn't going crazy?

The questions spun in her head as she pushed the big brass key into the lock and turned it. The click that followed sounded very loud to her, and the creak of the door as she pushed it open, even louder.

But the library during the day was like an entirely different room. It was bright, with sunlight pouring in through the windows, showing off tiny little dust motes floating in midair. Archie bounded into the room, his tail wagging, clearly much happier in the warmth of the summer day. Feeling braver, Emily hurried through the room. Even if the atmosphere was much different than last night, the bookshelves still felt threatening, after one had nearly crushed her.

Toward the back of the room, she came across the big mess. Except that she suspected either Miss Greer or Mr. Thornton tried to clean it up a little. The bookcase still lay splintered and cracked, but the books were stacked neatly in towers off to the side.

Seeing the broken furniture, though, brought the fresh memory straight to the surface.

She'd seen enough.

Emily rushed out of the library. "Archie!" she called as she got to the door. The dog ran to her side quickly and she turned and locked the door again.

Yes, the bookcase had indeed fallen. But she still had no idea if the moving shadows had been real.

Making sure her heart rate was normal, Emily hovered near the door until she heard a sound toward the end of the hallway.

Her heart leaping into her throat once again, Emily whipped her head in the direction of the sound. It had been metallic, not unlike a key fitting into a lock.

The corridor was long with few windows letting in daylight, so the gloom toward the end of the hall was concealing and mysterious. Emily wanted to back away, but she forced herself to move forward. It made her feel better that Archie wasn't whimpering or growling.

Three steps farther and she could see a shape; one step farther, and she could distinctly make out the form of a woman.

Emily gave a start. *Mrs. Thornton!*

But Emily had barely seen Mrs. Thornton beyond the first floor and a few rooms on the second floor, including her own. What was she doing so far back here?

The light shifted beyond the windows, making something in Mrs. Thornton's hands sparkle. In fluid movements, like Mrs. Thornton had done it a thousand times, she stuck the item in her hands into the door, turned it, then withdrew it and reached back, clasping the object around her neck.

For a moment, Emily was simply stunned. The strangely shaped pendant that Mrs. Thornton always wore and fiddled with was a *key.* She wasn't sure why she'd never realized it before. Maybe because it was so different from any other key she'd ever seen. But now that she thought about it, it had teeth like keys, and the size and shape were right.

Relieved that the mysterious figure hadn't been something else, Emily started down the hallway. "Mrs. Thorn— Mama!" She called.

Mrs. Thornton looked up, surprise sharpening her lovely, delicate features. Emily noticed immediately she didn't look as strong or as happy as she had the evening before, when they'd been going over Emily's wardrobe. Instead,

Mrs. Thornton was pale, with dark circles under her eyes.

"E-Emily, dear." Mrs. Thornton stumbled over Emily's name, her smile shaky as she looked down at her adopted daughter. "What are you doing up here? Haven't you had enough of this floor? I swear, it's as if everything is falling apart."

"What?" Emily asked. She hadn't even mentioned the well to Mrs. Thornton yet, but besides that and the bookshelf, what else was falling apart?

"Nothing to concern yourself with, dear." Leaning down, Mrs. Thornton patted her shoulder. "Come, let's steal a few almond scones with honey from Miss Greer. Doesn't that sound lovely?"

Of course Emily wouldn't say no to a treat like that, but she couldn't stop staring at the shiny skeleton key about Mrs. Thornton's swanlike neck. "Is that a key, ma'am? What does it open?"

The reaction was stronger than Emily had been expecting. Mrs. Thornton drew back, her thin hand clawing at the strange pendant and squeezing it tightly. "This is—It's a special key, Emily. I must always have it with me. Do you understand?"

Emily didn't understand, but Mrs. Thornton gripped her shoulder in a way that made it clear that no more questions should be asked.

The next day Emily didn't go on the third floor. In fact, she didn't explore the manor at all. She sat curled up in a chair in the scullery, watching Miss Greer cook. Occasionally she helped out with simple tasks like washing the vegetables or shucking the peas, but Miss Greer wouldn't let her do much more than that.

"Miss Emily, are you sure you don't have someplace else you'd rather go play?" Miss Greer asked for the fourth time.

The truth was that there were dozens of things she'd rather be doing and exploring. There were still easily fifty more rooms she hadn't seen—including, of course, the forbidden room at the end of the west wing on the third floor—but she also felt like there was a dark cloud of bad luck hovering over her head. She worried that whatever room she would visit, she'd break something or rip another one of her dresses. It was superstition, but she couldn't help but want to stay in the safety and the sunlight of Miss Greer's scullery.

That, and she feared the shadows lurking. Waiting for her, in her mind or in the house, she wasn't sure which. But she didn't want to see them again. Even her own room felt foreboding at times. Especially at night, when it would get so cold and the noises from the mysterious room above her would be loud enough for Emily to hear, but soft enough never to be sure what they were.

So Emily just shook her head and spent the day peaceful, albeit a little bored.

By the time supper rolled around, Miss Greer insisted that Emily not stay in the scullery the following day. She claimed young girls needed their exercise, but Emily suspected she was simply annoyed by all of Emily's questions and musings.

"The Thorntons will be visiting some friends tomorrow, so you will need to find another way to occupy yourself. And don't worry, Mrs. Thornton has already requested a governess, so come September you will have studies to attend to."

Emily wished that it was already September. It wasn't that she was excited to have a governess or studies again—not that she particularly minded them—but then it would mean that there was someone with her instead of being alone in this great old house that already seemed to dislike her.

Not that a house could have feelings.

Of course the thought crossed her mind to spend time with Kat, but the truth was that bad things seemed to happen with her nearby. It was as if Kat were a bad luck charm herself. Plus, she didn't know how to find Kat or even where she lived. The girl just seemed to pop up out of nowhere.

The following day, with Mr. and Mrs. Thornton off in

London visiting friends, and Miss Greer working on laundry, Emily and Archie sat in a drawing room a few doors down from Mr. Thornton's study. It was one of the few rooms in the whole house that wasn't covered head to foot in dust and cobwebs. According to Miss Greer, it was where Mrs. Thornton spent a lot of time doing embroidery and sketching. Emily had even found some paper and a charcoal pencil to use.

"Sit just there, Archie. Now stay," Emily commanded, signaling with her palm to make Archie stay.

But the lazy bones wasn't going anywhere. He was curled up in the middle of the rug with his eyes closed and was practically snoozing in the late-morning sunlight coming through the window.

Tongue between her teeth, Emily began to sketch the rough shape of Archie on the floor. A few minutes into her sketching, she realized she didn't have a talent for it at all.

Suddenly a voice said, "That's rubbish, isn't it?"

Nearly jumping up, Emily jerked around to find Kat

leaning over the back of the chair and looking at Emily's sketch with a small smirk.

Emily gave a nervous laugh as Archie lifted his head from the rug, a growl starting in his throat as his tail thumped heavily on the carpet.

"You startled me!"

"Maybe you were concentrating too hard, but I'm not surprised you didn't hear me. I'm quite good at sneaking up on people."

Emily didn't doubt it. Quickly, she tried to tuck away her awful drawing, knowing that Kat would make fun of it. But Kat was too fast and snatched the drawing away.

"Oh, yes, that's just dreadful," Kat critiqued.

Emily's cheeks grew warm and she scowled. "I know. It's my first time."

Kat handed her back the drawing with a thoughtful look. "Do you like art, Emily? Do you want to see some beautiful paintings?"

"Sure," Emily answered. She had her doubts, going

exploring with Kat again, but she knew that everything that had happened were just accidents and Emily couldn't blame her one and only human friend for a bunch of bad luck. Besides, she was rather excited at the prospect of seeing paintings. Even though Emily had rarely dealt with the arts like painting, music, or works of fiction, she'd always admired them and the people who could create them.

Getting up from the chair, Emily turned to Archie. "You coming, boy?"

"Leave him here," Kat instructed. "You don't want him to knock over anything that's priceless, do you?"

But Emily wanted Archie with her. She felt better with him by her side. So she folded her arms and frowned. "Archie will be fine. He's a good boy."

Kat waved her hand as if she couldn't care less. "Fine, fine. Bring him along, then, but don't say I didn't warn you."

Archie followed the two girls, and when Kat seemed to get too close to him, he would growl, his lips peeling back to show his teeth. Emily couldn't understand why he didn't like Kat so much. Maybe it was because Kat reminded him of someone from the orphanage or the streets of London who he didn't like. Whatever the reason, he kept his distance from her.

They walked through the manor for a long time, Emily following Kat down the hall of the first floor deeper into the west wing than Emily had ever been.

After Kat instructed Emily on which key to use, they entered the room at the very end of the hall. It had great big bay windows with sunlight shining through, highlighting all the dust motes dancing in the air. There were dozens of large portraits leaned up against the walls, covered with sheets, and columns with ceramic vases, and busts of older lords and ladies that must be ancestors of the Thorntons lined the walls. Maybe they were even the original owners of Blackthorn.

For a few minutes, Emily forgot Kat had come along with her and Archie. The room was quiet and so bright and beautiful, it was as if she'd entered another world all on her own. In somewhat of a daze, Emily drifted over to one of the largest portraits and started to pull back the sheet that covered it. Emily barely caught a glimpse of what looked like a young child on a rocking horse before Kat tugged the sheet back over it.

"Not that one!" she snapped, and then she pushed Emily toward another set of paintings. "Look at these."

Confused, but not wanting to get into an argument, Emily drew the sheet back on the other paintings. The sheet made a rustling sound as it slid away from the frames, and Emily could've sworn she heard a voice through the sound. *"Look here, Emily."*

But this time the voice didn't bother her. It was as if the paintings themselves were vying for her attention so she could admire their beauty. They were all oil paintings of forests, and they were absolutely magical. Big trees with large evergreen boughs, so grand and mighty that Emily would've bet that unicorns lived in those woods.

While she was absorbed in the artwork, completely enchanted by the rich colors, her fingers started to grow a little numb from the cold. Once again, the strange chill had returned, and Emily, startled at the sudden and intense drop in temperature, glanced around, about to ask Kat if she felt it, too.

Suddenly, Archie yipped in panic.

Emily turned to check on her friend just in time to see a massive ceramic vase just behind her wobble on its stand and then—

*CRAAAACK.*

Amazingly, Emily ducked out of the way at the exact last moment, but the vase still shattered, hitting the floor and bursting into a thousand pieces.

Emily stood there in shock for she wasn't sure how long, the room completely empty. Kat had vanished. Eventually, she became aware of Archie licking her hand and the footsteps and call of Miss Greer from down the hall.

Miss Greer burst into the room; took one look at the shattered vase, Emily, and Archie; and gasped, hands flying to her mouth. "Emily! What on earth—"

"Uh . . . u-um . . ." Emily stuttered. She couldn't speak.

The housekeeper glanced from her, then to Archie at Emily's side. "Emily, did Archie—"

"No!" Emily cried. "It was me, Miss Greer. I did it."

Miss Greer fixed Emily with a cold, level stare. "I see," she said slowly. "Go up to your room, Emily. Your parents will deal with you when they get home."

Needless to say, Emily spent most of the evening trying hard not to cry. She let a few sniffles escape here and there, which were more of a result of frustration than anything else. It wasn't her or Archie who had knocked over the vase, and yet she was going to get the blame for it. It was like being back at Evanshire's with Agatha all over again. Emily couldn't stand the unfairness of it all! And as much as she wanted to blame *someone*, she couldn't blame Kat, either. The girl had been nowhere to be seen when the vase fell over. How could she have run away so quickly if it had been her?

Even though she was frustrated, it didn't stop her from being terrified when there was a knock on her door that evening after an awkward and silent supper with Miss Greer.

It looked as if her parents were home at last. Would she get a beating? What would the Thorntons do to her?

"Emily?" Mrs. Thornton said softly as she entered the room.

Emily sat on the bed, with her arms around her legs and her chin tucked on top of her knees. "Yes, ma'am?"

Archie raised his head from the rug that he'd been lying on as Mrs. Thornton crossed to the bed and sat next to Emily.

"Miss Greer told me you broke a vase."

Emily didn't want to look at Mrs. Thornton, but from her tone, Emily couldn't tell if she was angry or disappointed. "Yes, ma'am. I'm very sorry, ma'am."

"Look at me, Emily."

Reluctantly, Emily looked up at her adoptive mother with red-rimmed eyes. Mrs. Thornton took Emily's cheeks in her hands and wiped away any lingering dampness with the pads of her thumbs. "Was it an accident?"

"Yes, ma'am."

"Then we must be more careful next time, mustn't we?"

Emily sniffed. "Yes, ma'am." Her voice was shaky, but she felt relief more than anything else.

"All right, dear."

Then Mrs. Thornton kissed her forehead and said kindly, "Accidents happen, darling. I forgive you. Now get on to bed."

Still somewhat in shock that a woman could be that kind and forgiving, Emily got into bed, and Mrs. Thornton tucked her in. She was still in a state of elated relief when Mrs. Thornton blew out the light and closed the door after her.

She was just beginning to fall asleep when her name was whispered through the darkness.

*"Emily . . ."*

Emily sat up in bed, heart pounding. "Who's there?" she called into the gloom.

Archie growled and jumped on the bed with Emily, standing over her protectively.

"It's me—Kat."

Emily squinted and she could see the small figure of a girl at the edge of the bed. "Kat?" she asked, getting out of the bed and letting her bare feet touch the cold, cold floor.

As she came around the bed, Archie glued to her side, she did in fact feel a presence, but she still couldn't make out a face. "I can't see you," Emily said.

Just as the words passed through her lips, the fireplace roared to life right next to her. The flames were so big and intense that the flying embers burned the hem of her nightgown. Emily gave a short cry of alarm and stumbled back, falling on her backside onto the rug. Archie licked her cheek and whined beside her.

In the light of the fire, Kat stood a few feet away and rushed over to Emily's side. "Emily! Are you all right?"

Blearily, Emily batted at the smoking holes in the hem of her gown and let Kat help her to her feet. "I . . . I think so."

"I wanted to come check on you, because I saw the vase."

Even in the heat of the roaring fire, Kat's hands were like ice. Emily extracted herself from the girl's grasp and stared in wonder at the fire, which had seemed to ignite all on its own. "I'm all right, I think. Thank you for checking on me."

Kat shook her head. "You need to be more careful, Emily."

Everyone seemed to be telling her that. The only problem was that she never saw a reason to be careful until it was too late.

Several days passed in a state of ups and downs. One moment, Emily couldn't believe her luck and happiness in finding a family such as the Thorntons, and then the next, she couldn't be more terrified.

There were . . . *things* happening throughout the Blackthorn estate. It was as if the house itself were rejecting Emily. The bookshelf almost crushing her, the well crumbling away beneath her, the vase almost falling on her head, and the fireplace suddenly flaring to a roar and nearly scorching her nightgown.

In all of these accidents, Kat never noticed a thing,

which led Emily to think that maybe it really *was* her imagination. But the bookshelf remained broken, the well half destroyed, the vase shattered to pieces . . . all those things were real. They happened.

And deep down, Emily knew the shadows were real, too.

She'd taken to calling them shadows even though they felt like more than that. They were alive—she just knew it. They called to her, haunted her nightmares, made Archie bark, growl, and snarl. She wanted to be as ferocious as her friend, but her courage failed her every time. When she thought she saw them wiggling in a dark corner, her blood would freeze and wouldn't thaw until Archie licked or nuzzled her frozen hand.

The forbidden room above her bedroom also made strange thumps and footsteps that made Emily's skin crawl. She could write off the footsteps as maybe the Thorntons walking around in their private room, but she sometimes heard soft weeping and, more than once, she saw the living shadows congregate on the ceiling in broad daylight when she was brushing her hair.

Then there were the giggles and the voices, too. Just small, distant whispers, so soft that many times Emily would ask herself if she'd heard anything at all. But then the cold would come and Emily would know that the words had *not* been inside her head.

"Emily? Emily, dear?"

Emily's head jerked downward. She'd been staring at a corner of the ceiling, far away from the chandelier light. She could have sworn she saw a moving shadow ripple across the molding.

Mr. Thornton sat to her left, frowning behind his dark mustache. "Emily, are you quite all right?"

She swallowed. The chicken she'd been chewing slid down her throat, a tasteless lump. "I'm fine."

"You don't look fine. Perhaps you should go to bed early tonight."

Emily glanced at Mrs. Thornton. She was moving food around on her plate, barely eating anything at all. She, too, looked pale and tired, but Mr. Thornton was maybe used to his wife looking like that.

“Yes, I think I’ll do that,” Emily said, her voice meek. She tried not to look back up at the ceiling.

“She probably hasn’t been getting a lick of sleep,” Miss Greer boomed, coming around behind Emily’s chair and dropping another steaming roll onto her plate, even though Emily clearly didn’t have an appetite.

Mr. Thornton’s frown deepened. “Why haven’t you been sleeping well, Emily?”

Before she could respond, Miss Greer waved her tongs at the master of Blackthorn Manor. “It’s that dog of hers! Getting up in the middle of the night, roaming around and scratching and whining. Why, I heard him just the other night whimpering away.”

“Hmm.” Mr. Thornton rubbed his whiskers. “Maybe we should keep him outside for a—”

“No!” Emily tried not to shout, but her voice was louder than it should ever be at the supper table. All three adults stared at her. “I mean . . . no, please. I’ll keep him in my room tonight. I’ll lock my door. It’ll be fine—I promise.”

Mr. Thornton glanced at his wife, then nodded as if the matter was settled.

That night, Emily stayed awake. She kept the candle going, and when Archie got up from the rug, slinking away toward her cracked door, she quietly got out of bed, grabbed the candle, and hurried after him.

She had to find out where her friend was going every night.

The dog moved through the house like he was hunting for something. She knew English pointers were a hunting breed, perfect for foxhunts. But having raised him from a pup, Emily knew he'd never hunted for sport. Besides catching the occasional rat at the orphanage, hunting wasn't something he did, although apparently it was bred into him.

As they mounted the stairs to the third floor, Emily grew colder. Once again, she wished she'd worn slippers or a robe, but it was too late to turn back now. She had to keep going no matter how terrified she was, and no matter how tight her stomach clenched.

At the top of the stairs, Archie stopped and sniffed the air. Then he bent his head and turned down the west wing. Emily's heart skipped a beat.

At the end of the hall was the forbidden room. The room that Archie had gone to their second day at the manor, and the room that seemed constantly to be at the edge of her thoughts. Maybe she should've guessed that it was that door Archie returned to every night. It was certainly the door that Emily was aching to be behind most. But she had kept her promise to the Thorntons. She'd made sure not to go there, regardless of how much she'd wanted to, regardless of how often she'd thought about whatever resided above the room in which she slept every night. Archie was moving toward it, continuing his hunt. She'd followed him for a reason tonight, and she couldn't go without finding out why.

Maybe it was nothing at all. Maybe a cat lived in that room and the Thorntons didn't want to show her.

Or maybe it was the source of the shadows and all the

coldness and whispers. Maybe it was the lair of the monster that was not supposed to exist.

*Go—it's just a room,* Emily told herself.

*Yes, and shadows are just shadows.*

Steeling herself, Emily followed Archie down the hall. From her candle's glow she could make out the state of the corridor, and it was awful. Wallpaper peeled at the tops, bottoms, and halfway down in the middle. The moldings looked black with, well, *mold.* Then there were large discolored patches on the wall in the shapes of portraits long since taken down. Maybe so they wouldn't be destroyed by the same ruin that seemed to have fallen upon the rest of the hall.

*"Turn back."*

Emily stopped, hearing the whisper echo in her ears, pinching her shoulders tight in fear. Could that be inside her head this time? Maybe it was her conscience—her fear manifesting into words that told her to stay away from the evil that lay ahead. But unlike the other times, instead of beckoning her forward, the voice was telling her to leave. Should she heed it? After all, whatever was whispering to her seemed to enjoy luring her into danger.

Maybe she should do the exact opposite this time.

Plus, she couldn't just leave Archie.

Emily's hands trembled as she followed Archie farther and farther down the corridor, making the candlelight beam jump and shake. Which, of course, didn't help the idea of shadows coming to haunt her.

With each step she wanted to turn back, just like the voice had said, but her feet carried her forward, her gaze locked on the door where Archie had stopped. He stood still, one paw up, nose down, pointing at the door's threshold.

Then a buzzing reached Emily's ears. It was very soft at first, then grew louder with each step. Her hands and skin turned colder. The seconds seemed to stretch as the buzzing morphed into whispers that prickled the hair on her arms. The voice whispered again, but this time, she couldn't make out the words. What was it saying?

Archie whined, scratching at the door, breaking through the whispers. Emily stood next to him now, transfixed by the sight of the door. It was . . . pristine. White and clean and beautiful—a stark contrast to the tragic state of the rest of the corridor.

This room was different.

As she reached for the door's handle, a freezing wind swept from underneath the door, blowing out her candle and lifting the hair off her shoulders. The whispering came back like a roar, loud as a thousand voices trying to speak out at once—each one vying for her attention.

It was completely dark, and at any moment she felt like the shadows would come and devour her. But she knew where the door was. She knew its handle was inches from her fingers. Utterly terrified, yet strangely compelled, Emily grasped the door handle.

It was like touching ice.

The whispering vanished, silent for a beat, and then:

"*GET. OUT.*"

The shrill words blasted through Emily like an ocean wave in a storm. She was on the ground, skidding across the damp old carpet.

Archie barked and ran toward her, growling and snarling at nothing at all. Except Emily knew there was something. Something evil and filled with hate.

Emily scrambled to her feet and ran with Archie back down the hall to the staircase, not looking back—not *ever* looking back.

Emily ran down the hall like there was a monster after her. With everything she'd seen and heard, it probably *was* a monster. Regardless of what it was, she just knew she had to get away. If she could, she'd run out of this manor all the way back to London to escape whatever evil thing lay beyond that door.

Just as Emily rounded the corner to the grand staircase, she collided with a pair of legs. Falling onto her backside with Archie whining and licking at her cheeks, she looked up, still shaking terribly, to see Mrs. Thornton standing above her, holding a gaslit lantern.

"Emily?" Her voice was high and wavering in the vast silence of the manor.

Now that Emily had stopped running, she was finally aware of how quiet it all was.

"What are you doing up here? Why are you out of bed again?" she asked, looking down at Emily, then stepping around the corner and lifting up her lantern to cast a sphere of golden light down the haunted hall.

*Haunted.*

Could that be what it was? Were all of these incidents—the shadows, the decay, the chill, the objects falling—the work of some kind of evil spirit?

She remembered the girls at the orphanage telling ghost stories as a way to pass the time. She'd never paid much attention to them. She preferred her stories of fairy tales and princesses and knights, not of poltergeists and tales of murder.

Of course, the idea that this was all the work of some ghost was somehow even more frightening than a monster.

A monster felt imaginary. A ghost . . . a ghost felt real.

"Emily? Emily dear, what *is* it?" Mrs. Thornton pressed, bending down and taking Emily's shoulder and squeezing it.

"I . . . I . . . There was . . ." Emily could barely speak. Fear took hold of her throat and was squeezing it much too tightly to get any words out. How could she tell her new mother that she believed a ghost lived at the end of the hall? No, best only to tell her mother what she'd experienced. Despite everything, she didn't want to leave her new parents and her new home, no matter how scary it was. And if she claimed that a ghost had been haunting her, they may think her mad enough to return her to Evanshire's.

"I—I was f-following A-Archie," Emily stuttered. "He stopped at a door at the end of the wing, and the door was all white and pretty. But the hallway is so awful-looking." She was talking faster and faster to make sure all the words got out before she lost her nerve again. Archie nuzzled her hand. Wrapping her arm around his neck, she drew strength and comfort from his warm body and continued onward. "And then there was all this buzzing—like a bunch of voices whispering at me. Then it suddenly got really, really cold and there was a big gust of wind and—"

"Charlotte?" Mr. Thornton came up the steps in a dark green robe, holding a candle, and when his gaze went from his wife to his new daughter, his brow furrowed in either anger or confusion. "Emily? What the devil is going on here?"

"Robert!" Mrs. Thornton exclaimed, gripping the key around her neck tight in her fist. She looked desperately at her husband, then glanced back down the hall. The lantern she was holding was trembling. Trembling so hard the light beams jumped around, making the shadows once again look alive.

Emily shivered, wrapping both arms around Archie this time.

Mr. Thornton seemed to understand his wife's reaction better than Emily did, because he turned to Emily and gave her a look angrier than she'd ever seen from him. "Emily, what are you doing out of bed?" There was an iciness to his words.

Quickly, Emily repeated what she'd just told Mrs. Thornton. "Then there was this really big gust of wind and my candle went out and it was all dark and then—"

"Enough!" Mr. Thornton shouted. His voice was so loud it echoed throughout the manor, carrying through the wings and down the staircase.

Emily shrank back from her adoptive father and felt Archie growl. Any trace of Mr. Thornton's kindness from the past few days was gone.

"I will hear no more of this nonsense. It was just a bad draft and your childish imagination," he snapped. "I *told* you—no more nighttime escapades. I expect you to keep your promises, Emily. We gave you those keys because we trust you, and now you've betrayed that trust by going back on your word."

"I—I'm sorry," Emily murmured, tears springing to her eyes. She felt weak and silly for crying again. But the monster—the ghost—*whatever*—had scared her senseless, and now the Thorntons didn't believe her. Not only that, but Mr. Thornton was exactly right: She'd betrayed their trust. He had every right to be angry at her.

Even so, Emily knew what she'd seen and what she'd felt. It wasn't her imagination anymore. There was no need for doubt. It was real. Although she'd been terrified, and disobeyed her father's orders, she didn't regret going to the third-floor west wing. She was relieved to know that it all wasn't in her head.

It didn't make her feel much better. In fact, it just made her cry harder. It probably also had something to do with the fact that she'd made Mr. Thornton yell at her. Miss Evanshire had yelled at her constantly, and she'd never once cried—or really cared, for that matter. But now that it was Mr. Thornton, a man whom she respected and cared for . . . suddenly, it made all the difference in the world.

As Emily sniffled and hung her head, trying to wipe her tears away with her sleeve, she sensed Mr. Thornton take a step toward her, then bend down on one knee, dropping to her level.

She peeked up from the crevice of her elbow to see that Mr. Thornton's face had changed to one of concern. "Now, now, my dear. There's no need for tears. I think we're all just a little stressed over the bad luck that's been following us around. I think what we need is some life in this house, a little celebration." He brushed Emily's unruly dark hair away from her face and tucked it affectionately behind her ear.

Emily was too stunned to reply. Going from yelling to suggesting a celebration was entirely different than Miss Evanshire's way of scolding children.

"A party, Robert?" Mrs. Thornton seemed equally surprised. She also kept glancing back down the hall as if she expected someone or something to come walking out of the shadows. Her hand still clutched the key at her throat like it was her most precious thing in the world.

Mr. Thornton stood and looped a strong arm about his wife's waist and took the lantern from her shaking hands.

"Yes, Charlotte. I think it would be good for us. We've never really celebrated Emily joining our family, not officially, anyway. We should have one in her honor, don't you think?"

Mrs. Thornton looked over her shoulder at the dark hallway, then back at her husband's face. Biting her bottom lip, her fingers slowly loosened their hold on her necklace. "Yes, I think we should do it."

"It's settled," Mr. Thornton said with a nod, then he kissed his wife's forehead. "Well, let's get back to bed. It's the middle of the night and now we have much to do. I'll talk to Miss Greer first thing tomorrow morning."

Mr. Thornton guided Mrs. Thornton back toward the stairs, and as they started down them, Emily, too, took one more look at the hallway. She was terrified, but just like how she'd reached for the door, Emily was oddly compelled to look even though she felt as if she'd never want to again.

If her eyes weren't deceiving her, she could've sworn something moved within the darkness. This time, though, it wasn't just the shadows wiggling and twitching against the walls. It was a dark shape, like a figure or a silhouette.

Archie growled and tugged at her nightgown.

Unfreezing from her terror, Emily turned and ran down the stairs to catch up to the light of the Thorntons' lantern and the warmth of their company.

That whole week, poor Miss Greer was worked to the bone preparing for Emily's welcome party. It was a strain that she put on herself, however, since Mr. and Mrs. Thornton insisted that she need not trouble herself with the extra work.

The Thorntons didn't seem to care much about the dust and the cobwebs and the ruin of the house in general. It was as if they were impervious to seeing the true state of their home, the dire shape it was in.

The second day of Miss Greer's attack on the house with a mop, broom, and duster, Emily asked the housekeeper why she was working so hard if the Thorntons didn't ask her to. To Emily, it seemed like she had plenty of work already without the added labor of cleaning the entire first floor from head to foot.

"I won't let the guests see the manor in such a state," Miss Greer fussed as she dragged buckets of soapy water to the dining hall and the main entrance to wash every corner of the floor.

Emily rolled up the sleeves of her smock and dunked her sponge into the soapy water. "Why don't the Thorntons hire more help? It's clearly too much work for one person."

Miss Greer gave her a warm smile, then sighed and shook her head. "Grief will make a person blind, and it will drive away others, even when you need them most."

"What do you mean? Why are they sad?" Emily took the sponge out of the bucket and big droplets of soapy water fell onto her apron. Could there be a very important reason behind Mrs. Thornton's strange mood swings? Was it not her health at all, but her heart?

Miss Greer paled a little in the warm yellow glow of the hall and pressed her lips together in a thin line. Wagging a finger at Emily, she said, "No one likes a nosy child, Miss Emily. Now, this floor isn't going to scrub itself."

Still curious, but knowing that Miss Greer wasn't going to say anything more, Emily went back to her task. Even if it was cleaning, she was glad to have something to do while her parents hardly paid any attention to her.

Mr. Thornton locked himself in his study and Mrs. Thornton kept to her room. Occasionally, Emily would sneak past her mother's room to see her sitting on a large chair by the fire, not even lit, fiddling with her necklace. She'd just sit there, staring at the ash and remnants of burnt wood, her fingers rubbing the metal teeth of the odd skeleton key about her neck.

While the Thorntons were distracted and aloof, Emily helped Miss Greer clean. She didn't mind the chores one bit. In fact, she welcomed the busyness of the routine. It helped keep her mind off the fact that a ghost was hiding up in the corner of the manor. Spending time with Miss Greer helped drive away the evil chill and the whispering voices. It was as if working in the sunlight with another person warded off the evil spirits, or at least made it harder for them to appear.

Also, while helping Miss Greer clean, Emily saw less and less of Kat. The girl only showed up when Emily was completely alone, and as soon as Miss Greer called for Emily, Kat would run off.

Even though many of her adventures with Kat had been fun, they had also been dangerous somehow. So she was both relieved and only a little bit disappointed when Kat would leave and Emily was left to her chores.

At night, Emily had Archie sleep in her bed with her, not caring about dog hair in the sheets, and she had multiple candles going to help drive away the shadows.

They helped, but she wondered how much longer she could keep this up. She wouldn't be able to sleep with Archie every night or work with Miss Greer all day long.

At some point she would have to be on her own, and what would happen then?

Emily was scared to think of it.

The morning of the party, Mrs. Thornton herself came in to wake up Emily. The shocking presence of her new mother was enough to wake her out of her sleepy daze, and she sat up in bed with Archie still tucked under her sheets, his tail thumping.

Mrs. Thornton smiled pleasantly and deposited a breakfast tray on the vanity seat. "Good morning, dear. I thought we'd have a little breakfast together."

Still trying to shake off her surprise, Emily crawled out of her covers to sit on the edge of her bed.

"Um, thank you, Mama."

Mrs. Thornton beamed at that and gracefully poured Emily a cup of tea. As Emily accepted the cup, Archie's head popped out from under the covers, and he panted happily at the sight of another person.

Laughing, Mrs. Thornton shook her head. "Oh, dear, we

best not tell Miss Greer about that. She won't be too pleased at Archie's sleeping arrangements."

Emily smiled at Mrs. Thornton's good mood. Was it because of the party tonight?

They ate breakfast in a comfortable silence, and once they were done, Mrs. Thornton gestured to the vanity. "Take a seat, Emily, and let me do your hair."

Emily practically ran to the cushioned stool in front of the mirror. She didn't bother suppressing her grin as Mrs. Thornton picked up the brush and began to comb through Emily's crazy bedhead hair. She'd always imagined her real mother brushing her hair and fixing it up into some lovely, fancy curls. It had seemed like such a distant dream to Emily, but now here she was.

As Mrs. Thornton worked on her hair, twisting it and tucking it with pins, Emily watched her concentrated face in the mirror.

With Emily's thick hair, it took all of the morning and into the afternoon, and Emily was tired of sitting, but it was worth it. Her curls looked heavenly, and

Mrs. Thornton seemed just as pleased with the end result. After picking out a new dark blue dress for Emily to wear to the party, Mrs. Thornton left to get ready herself.

As soon as the door closed behind her, a large thump came from above.

Emily and Archie froze at the sound. Slowly, Emily raised her head to look at the ceiling and gasped, her blood running as cold as freshly melted snow.

Darkness streaked all across the ceiling, like black paint spilled against white. It reached the moldings and dripped down the walls.

Right near her ear, the voice whispered, *"Don't act so conceited."*

Emily lifted cold, shaking hands to her lips, and the darkness reached the carpet and inched toward her. Getting closer and closer.

Archie whined, then let a deep growl rip through his throat, followed by a sharp bark.

All week, Emily hadn't seen anything reminding her of the ghost, but now, after Mrs. Thornton had spent all morning with her, it was like the ghost was back—and it was even angrier than before.

Emily didn't wait a second longer. She ran out of her room, Archie at her side, and slammed the door behind her. Pulling out her key ring, she locked her door with trembling fingers.

Her heartbeat thundered in her ears, and her breath was like a wind tunnel. Her whole body was shaking. She knew she wouldn't be going back to her room today—or maybe ever again.

Until the party, Emily stayed in the scullery with Miss Greer. She enjoyed watching the old housekeeper cook, but more than anything she was there for the warmth of the fires and the chatter of company to chase away the chill and silence of the fear that still had hold of her.

Even Archie was subdued. The English pointer mix lay under her chair, shaking every so often. Miss Greer was nice enough to feed him scraps, but she wouldn't let Emily try a bite.

"You'll ruin your supper," she said.

Emily was fine with that. She didn't have much of an appetite anyway.

When the guests started to arrive, one of the last things she wanted to do was go and meet them and smile like everything was all right, but as Miss Greer reminded her, it was *her* party, after all.

There were many fine ladies and gentlemen in sharp suits and beautiful gowns, but no children. Emily thought it silly that although Mr. Thornton had claimed the party was for her, very few of the guests seemed to pay her any mind, and none of the guests were her age.

But Mrs. Thornton was lovely. She wore a dark red satin dress with jewels glittering at her neck and her hair wound up in curls. Like that morning, Mrs. Thornton seemed different than she had in the first couple weeks of Emily's time at Blackthorn. Her smile was bright and relaxed, and she looked . . . happy.

It was then she realized that this party wasn't for Emily

at all. It was for Mrs. Thornton. Emily didn't know the reason as to why Mrs. Thornton had been so melancholy, but it was clear from her significant change in mood that this party was meant to cheer up Mrs. Thornton more than to introduce Emily to society.

Knowing that, it made Emily want to try harder to make this dinner a success. She wanted her new mother to be in brighter spirits, and if there was anything she could do to make it better, she would try—even if that meant trying to forget, at least for an evening, that she lived in the same house as a ghost.

As Emily watched the Thorntons move from guest to guest, talking and laughing, she noticed Mrs. Thornton's hand would lightly graze the jewels at her neck, and that was when Emily realized: This was the first time she'd seen Mrs. Thornton without the skeleton key necklace.

Did that mean anything?

Sure, the ruby and diamond jewels matched her scarlet dress much better than the key, but the way Mrs. Thornton was always fiddling with the blasted thing, Emily had assumed it was very dear to her.

She put the thought out of her mind. It didn't matter tonight. Besides, she wanted to focus on all of her manners, on being a proper lady. All of her schooling at Miss Evanshire's was finally going to pay off.

Standing by Mr. Thornton, Emily took a deep breath and prepared herself. When she appeared at his elbow, he paused, smiled down at her, and then introduced her to a lord and lady from a manor in Brighton.

"Emily—a lovely name and an even lovelier dress," the woman said kindly. The man simply nodded at her.

"Thank you, my lady," Emily responded politely.

But that was all that was addressed to her, and soon the rest of the conversation carried into politics. Apparently Mr. Thornton's uncle was in parliament and a new law had been passed, and so it went on and on.

Emily tried to pay attention but her focus was quickly fading. Seeing an opening when the gentleman remarked on his appetite, Emily interjected, "I'll go check on supper," and then excused herself.

As she was moving past the guests, she couldn't help but overhear a snippet of conversation.

"She's so . . . different. Complete opposite of . . . you know."

"Indeed. But she's tall for a twelve-year-old, and her hair is so dark."

"Practically black!"

"I can't blame them, of course. Not after what happened."

"*Hush!* Here she comes."

The women moved away from Emily. Their voices were too low to hear anything else, and it would be too obvious if Emily followed them, but she was so curious! It was obvious to Emily that they were comparing her to someone, but whom?

Emily was still thinking about this when she exited the room and emerged into the hall, almost running into Miss Greer and a young maid they'd hired to help serve the guests.

"Miss Emily!" The housekeeper lifted her silver tray, scowling down at her. "Do watch where you're going!"

"Sorry, Miss Greer. When will supper be ready?"

"We're putting out the dishes now. You should go find a seat, if you like." The housekeeper nodded toward the dining room, but Emily didn't yet move.

"Can I help?" she asked.

"Yes, go make sure Archie is out of the dining room. I thought I saw him go in there."

"Yes, ma'am." Emily hurried through the large double doors and scanned the dining room for signs of her friend.

It was beautifully decorated. Clearly all their hard work had paid off. Candelabras lined the walls, standing guard over the windows like fiery knights. Silverware glimmered in the light, and fine china sets were laid out in perfect symmetry across a pure white tablecloth.

"Archie," Emily hissed, crouching down and lifting up the tablecloth.

Sure enough, Archie lay underneath one chair, his tail curled around its leg. He opened one eye lazily at his name, then closed it again as if he couldn't be bothered to move.

"Archie, c'mon, boy!"

"Miss Emily! Get up now, the guests are coming!" Miss Greer snapped as she entered the dining room.

"But—" Emily didn't have time to explain because the first few guests trickled into the dining room.

From the look on Miss Greer's face, she knew that Archie would be in trouble if he showed himself in a dining room with all these guests, so all Emily could do was hope that Archie napped throughout the whole dinner. Which, of course, he wouldn't. Not with all the food they were about to have.

Quickly, Emily went to take the seat that Archie lay under and waited nervously for the rest of the guests and the Thorntons to arrive.

To her great relief, Archie stayed quiet throughout the first course, and by the time the third course came out, Emily had almost entirely forgotten he was there.

This was partly thanks to the fact that the lord and lady whom she'd been talking to earlier with Mr. Thornton sat next to her and began asking Mrs. Thornton questions about Emily.

"Emily's dress is just divine, Charlotte. Where did you get it?"

Mrs. Thornton smiled from across the table at Emily and dabbed her lips with her napkin. "Oh, Miss Pinkerton is a dear friend of the family, and she had some delightful new fabrics to try out. Emily, tell Lady Brining about your other dresses and which one you like best."

Emily was about to respond when a whine came from under her chair.

*Archie!* Thinking that she would pretend to drop her napkin and shush Archie, Emily paused and glanced away from the lord and lady to see—

*Kat?!*

Emily's mouth popped open—thankfully with no food—and watched as Kat emerged from behind the drapes, as if she'd been there the whole time. But that couldn't be right. Surely someone would've noticed . . . right?

Kat caught Emily's eye and smiled that same cruel little smirk, pressing a single finger to her lips.

“Emily?” Mrs. Thornton prompted, frowning at the shocked look on Emily’s face and her stunned silence.

Kat turned, whipping the drapes back around her, and vanished into their folds.

Then many terrible things happened at once.

From the moldings and crevices of the ceiling, the black shadows dripped down the walls like sludge. The curtains blew from a gust of cold wind, or rippled as if someone had just run behind them. Emily watched with horror as a candelabra floated up, hovering in the air between two sets of the dark green drapes. It tilted purposefully, stabbing its candle flames into the fabric.

As the flames caught hold of the curtains, Archie gave a sharp bark from underneath her chair, and the guests all looked up from their food, many dropping their utensils and napkins in surprise.

The bark shook Emily out of her trance, and she leaned across the table, pointing at the growing inferno.

“Fire!” she cried.

Twisting in their seats to look behind them, the adults

all gave shouts and cries of surprise. The fire roared against the curtains, growing stronger and spreading faster than was natural. It was as if something was fueling the fire, each spark and ember a manifestation of the rage and hate that Emily had felt at the end of that third-floor hallway.

*GET OUT.* It was almost as if Emily could hear those words through the crackle of the flames. Whispering to her. Screaming at her.

Despite the obvious danger and terror, Mr. Thornton and the rest of the men immediately jumped to action, pulling off their jackets and using them to smother the fire.

Smoke filled the air. All the women rushed out of the room, coughing and pressing handkerchiefs to their mouths. Mrs. Thornton grabbed Emily and dragged her out of the room, clutching her shoulders with trembling hands.

In that moment, Emily could see a looped chain around Mrs. Thornton's wrist: Dangling from the silver chain was the skeleton key. She hadn't taken it off after all; she'd merely made it into a bracelet instead. Briefly, Emily wondered if the day would ever come when her mother would take it off, and what it would mean when she finally did.

Archie stood guard next to her, panting from the sudden heat and the thick smoke that clouded the air.

With the men beating out the flames using the other curtains they'd ripped down and their ruined, burnt jackets, the fire was reduced to nothing more than ash. But through all the chaos, the women crying, the men yelling, and Mrs. Thornton squeezing her, Emily could hear a giggle, clear as day, right next to her ear . . .

Once all the guests had left, Mr. Thornton came into the scullery, where Mrs. Thornton, Miss Greer, and Emily all sat sipping tea. Or rather, they weren't so much sipping their tea as clutching at their cups and staring at nothing. Miss Greer had her arm around Mrs. Thornton, rubbing small circles on her back, while Mrs. Thornton tugged and tugged at the jewel necklace around her neck, her eyes wide and unseeing.

Archie's head lay in Emily's lap and Emily was stroking his ears absentmindedly, trying to suppress the fresh waves of fear that washed over her every few minutes.

She did look up, however, when Mr. Thornton walked in, his face and nice white shirt covered in soot. Even the fringes of his fine mustache looked a little burnt. His appearance might've been a little funny if not for the look on his face.

He was staring at Emily and Archie with wild eyes and a deep-set frown.

"Emily," he said, his voice heavy and loud in the silence of the room, "what the devil happened at dinner?" His hands were clenched at his side.

Emily blinked, terrified not only at the ghost's malevolence but also at her adoptive father's barely restrained anger. She swallowed and tried to put forth words. After seeing the floating candelabra, there was not a doubt in her mind now that the manor was haunted. But how could she tell them that she believed there was a ghost at Blackthorn?

"I . . . I . . . The candles . . ."

At Emily's stuttering, Mr. Thornton seemed to get even more frustrated and he darted forward, grabbing Archie by the scruff of his collar. Archie gave a whimper but didn't protest or growl when Mr. Thornton dragged him away from Emily's lap.

"Was it this mutt? Did he knock over the candles?"

"What? No!" Emily cried, leaping from her chair and planting her feet squarely apart to face her father. "Archie didn't do it!"

"What else could have done it?" Mr. Thornton snapped.

"A ghost!" Emily yelled back.

The Thorntons and Miss Greer froze, staring at Emily with wide, horrified eyes.

A few seconds passed by in complete silence, Mr. Thornton opening and closing his mouth. Finally, he sputtered, "Don't be ridiculous."

"I'm not! There's a ghost haunting this manor, Mr. Thornton. Can't you feel it? It's been doing all sorts of things since I got here!" While the grown-ups continued to stare at Emily, she found her mouth moving faster and her words flowing out more panicked and higher than usual. "Tonight the candle stand lifted and floated *all on its own*! But other things happened even before that. It started with the bookshelf in the library that fell over. I saw all these moving shadows and then all of a sudden the bookshelf fell on its own. And then in the garden, the clovers and the flowers all wilted and died and the stones of the well crumbled and I almost fell in! There was another time when a vase almost fell on my head, and the fireplace suddenly turned on, and then when I went down the corridor, the door at the end *yelled* at me! It told me to get out!"

By the time Emily finished, she was panting as if she'd just finished running a mile.

It felt like hours before anyone said anything. The silence was interrupted only by a sob from Mrs. Thornton. Big crystal tears flowed down her cheeks as she threw herself into Miss Greer's arms. The housekeeper patted her on the back, shushing her in soft, comforting tones.

When Mr. Thornton finally talked again, his voice was hoarse and shaky.

"Emily, this level of disrespect will not be tolerated.

I did not expect you to be a disobedient child with such a wild imagination. Miss Evanshire warned us, but—"

Ignoring the sting of his words, Emily cried, "But it's all true!"

"Rubbish!" he hollered back, now shaking with rage. "These incidents were nothing more than accidents caused by your mutt." Without waiting for Emily's reply, he turned and began pulling Archie toward the basement door. "Archie will sleep in the basement until he can learn to behave. And you will go to bed immediately. No sweets and no roaming around the manor until *you* learn how to behave as well, and not tell such wicked lies."

Stunned into speechlessness, Emily could only watch as Mr. Thornton guided Archie down into the basement and slammed the door behind him.

Over Mrs. Thornton's crying form, Miss Greer said softly, "Off to bed with you now, Miss Emily. Best to let this whole mess die down. Things will be better in the morning, you'll see."

But Emily was quite sure that wouldn't be true. As she

made her way up the steps to her room, remembering the tangible shadows on the ceiling, she wondered how she'd ever make it through the night.

Something had to change, or else this ghost wouldn't stop until Emily never saw the light of another morning.

Up in her room, Emily paced the floor. With each step, her heart seemed to beat faster. She feared that if she looked up at the ceiling, it would be covered in wriggling black shadows. Every second that passed was a second that brought this ghost closer to her.

More than that, though, she couldn't stop thinking about her best friend locked in the basement all alone.

Of course, it wasn't Archie's fault—it was the ghost's! But she could understand Mr. Thornton's desperate need to pin all of these strange happenings on *something*. It made sense that he would use a dog as an excuse to explain the actions of a ghost, rather than admit that they were being haunted.

Even so, Emily couldn't let her friend stay down in the basement. She would free him—tonight—and then confront this ghost.

But how could she do that? It's not like the ghost had made any attempt to really contact her, other than to tell her to get out. Emily stopped pacing, hugging her arms to keep the chill out of her bones, and stared at the rug under her feet.

The ghost had told her to get out only when she'd touched the door upstairs. It was the mysterious room—the only room in the house that she'd never been allowed entrance. Mr. Thornton had told her not to go because it meant something to both him and Mrs. Thornton—that Emily should respect their privacy.

But it was also clearly the source of the ghost. That room held the answers to everything, and she could no longer keep her promise. The time for secrets was over.

If this evening's events were any indication, the ghost

was still here, it was angry, and it was only going to get worse and worse. The spirit that resided beyond that pristine white door amidst the rest of the decayed and ruined hallway wanted Emily out of the manor. For good.

Until tonight, she hadn't given much thought as to whose spirit it could be. Had it been someone who'd died at Blackthorn Manor? A ghost that hated Emily for some reason? But why? What had Emily done, aside from just coming to live here?

For the first time, Emily wished she would've paid attention to all those ghost stories the girls at Evanshire's told. She'd give anything to know how to get rid of a ghost—if it was even possible.

Maybe she just needed to find out the history of Blackthorn Manor. But who would tell her? She couldn't very well ask Mr. or Mrs. Thornton, and she doubted Miss Greer would give her any information. Maybe Kat would know, since she seemed to know everything else about the estate.

*Kat.*

Emily gasped and her hands flew to her mouth. With all the chaos of the fire and Mr. Thornton's anger, she had completely forgotten that Kat had been in the room mere seconds before the candles shoved themselves into the curtains. The little girl had disappeared into the folds of the fabric, but Emily knew that Kat must've escaped. Mr. Thornton would've said otherwise. There would have been a lot of fuss if they'd found an extra girl hiding in the drapes and the flames.

It was so strange how Kat seemed to be around when all of these bad things had happened. Or rather, she was around *just before* the bad things happened.

Emily didn't know if that was a coincidence or not, but if it wasn't, she had a lot of things she wanted to ask Kat. Maybe she should've bugged Kat about the history of Blackthorn Manor much sooner. Maybe she should've gone out to find her as soon as she discovered the ghost in the room down the third-floor west wing.

Unconsciously, she glanced up at the ceiling. It was still bare, but that didn't mean the shadows weren't on their way. And it didn't mean that they wouldn't show up later in the middle of the night while she was sleeping and slide down the walls, inching toward her bed . . .

Emily shivered, hugging her arms tighter and clenching her jaw. She had to find out what was inside.

But first things first: She had a best friend to rescue.

Emily wrenched open the door to her room and found her path blocked by none other than the very person who had disappeared during the fire. It was almost as if she'd been summoned by Emily's thoughts.

"Kat?" Emily gasped.

The girl slipped into Emily's room, jumping onto the bed and swinging her legs gleefully.

"That fire was just *awful*, wasn't it?" she said with a giggle.

"Yes," Emily replied coolly. "It was."

"It was a good thing everyone got out in time."

But Kat looked far too happy in the wake of something so scary. An awful feeling began to grab hold of Emily's insides and make its way up her spine.

"Kat," Emily repeated, taking a couple steps toward the girl. "What were you doing at dinner? People could've seen you."

Kat shrugged. "I was hiding in the curtains. No one but you saw."

"Did you see how the fire got started?"

Kat's smile faltered, her lips turning slowly downward into a scowl. "No, how could I? I was *hiding in the curtains*."

"But how did you get out?"

"Why are you asking me all these pointless questions, Emily?" Kat snapped.

"Because," Emily began slowly, thinking back to all the times something bad had happened in the house and Kat had been right nearby, "I think you had something to do with the fire."

Kat's hands squeezed the bedsheets, her frame as still

as a statue. She regarded Emily with cold eyes. "That's a serious accusation, Emily."

"There's a ghost in Blackthorn, Kat," Emily said, returning Kat's own stubbornness with her own. "And since you know everything about this manor, I think you *know* there's a ghost. And I think you're helping it somehow."

Emily didn't know how it was possible, but she was sure of it now. Kat had something to do with the ghost and all its evildoings. Maybe that was the reason Archie didn't like her, the reason he growled whenever Kat drew too close. Emily knew animals were more intuitive than humans about those kinds of things.

Kat's scowl broke into a wide grin and she threw her head back, laughing. "Oh, Emily," she said between giggles, "you have no idea what you're talking about."

Emily couldn't stand Kat's smugness or her mischievousness a second longer. "I'm going to tell the Thorntons about you."

At Emily's declaration, Kat stiffened. She jumped off

the bed, stalked toward Emily, and snarled, "You'll regret this."

Then she left the room, slamming the door behind her.

---

It took Emily a few minutes to calm down after the argument with Kat. With Kat's threat still lingering in the air, Emily decided not to bring a candle or a lantern with her, just in case. She also didn't know if Kat really did have any control over this terrible ghost, but she felt as if they had to be connected somehow. Like it all linked back to that forbidden room. And while the idea of moving through the hallway without at least a little bit of light was terrifying, the thought of starting yet another fire was unthinkable. She didn't want to put anyone else at risk.

The corridors seemed to stretch on forever. She padded quietly across the carpet, as fast as she dared. She didn't know what triggered the ghost's anger, so she just had to do as little as possible to not set off any ghostly alarms.

Keeping one hand on the walls, she dragged her fingers across the wallpaper, sure every second that she would brush against the shadows creeping down the inky blackness of the walls. But there was nothing. When she reached the banister to the stairs, she was happy to see at least a little better. Moonlight came in from the windows, streaming down in silver beams, illuminating the grand staircase and entrance hall with a soft gray light. It wasn't as warm and comforting as the sun would have been, but at least there was some light to see.

The stairs seemed to creak much louder than they had any other time she used them, and the squeaking noise echoed from the large, empty room. Emily froze on the middle landing, waiting for something to happen. For the shadows to come at her like black pythons. For the temperature to drop and freeze her hands and feet. For the chandelier to drop and shatter into a million pieces of crystal glass. *Something.*

But nothing came. All was still.

So Emily breathed a small sigh of relief and quickened her pace down the steps. Get to the basement. Get to Archie. Confront this ghost. Prove to the Thorntons that she wasn't crazy and that she appreciated their kindness. She wanted to keep staying here, after all. She didn't want a ghost to chase her away from the only family she'd ever come to know.

When she finally reached the scullery, Emily already felt like her nerves were shot and her heartbeat couldn't take it anymore. How would she ever survive the rest of the night?

But the sound of scratching and whining from beyond the basement door fueled her with renewed energy and determination. Tiptoeing across the stones of the scullery floor, Emily tried the basement door. It was locked.

Luckily, Mr. Thornton hadn't yet taken away her brass ring of keys. It took a little longer to find the right key because her hands were shaking so bad, but eventually one slid into the lock, and it made a loud click. Emily flinched at the sound and held her breath, waiting, once again, for something else to happen. For knives to hover above the table. For Miss Greer's pots to float over and fall on her head. But there was nothing.

Releasing another breath, Emily opened the door and carefully stepped onto the basement's steps. The basement wasn't very deep, so luckily there weren't many stairs. And to Emily's immense relief, there were quite a few windows that looked out to the garden at the top, so plenty of moonlight streamed in.

A few feet away from the bottom of the stairs sat a big metal cage with Archie inside. As soon as he saw her, he put his large paws up on the metal wires and whined, his nails scratching at the wiring uselessly.

"Shush, boy," Emily whispered. "I'm coming!" Trying not to trip, Emily went down the stairs as fast as she could and fell to her knees in front of Archie's crate.

As Emily wrapped her hands around the wiring, Archie licking her cheeks and fingers, she couldn't help but be reminded of her last night at Evanshire's Home for Neglected Girls, before the Thorntons had come the following morning. She and Archie had been separated by bars then, too. Were they better off at the orphanage? At least Evanshire's didn't have a murderous ghost.

*No.* Emily thought about Mr. Thornton giving her *Alice in Wonderland* and playing fetch with Archie, and Mrs. Thornton laying out dresses and curling her hair. These were wonderful, sweet people who did care for her.

She *belonged* here.

"We belong here, Archie," Emily said aloud, petting the top of his head and then scratching underneath his chin. Archie's big brown eyes looked up at her longingly, and he licked her palm affectionately.

"Now let's get you out," Emily said, turning around to inspect the rest of the basement. It wasn't like she had a key that went to this cage. She had a feeling that Mr. Thornton kept it with him. But there had to be something in this basement that could help her get Archie out.

As her gaze traveled across the room a second time, a bit more desperately, she finally noticed a work counter covered with old, rusty tools. Like the rest of the house and the grounds, she expected that these tools had lain for a long time gathering cobwebs. But something there might work despite the obvious age and disuse.

She crossed to the counter and blew off a thick layer of dust. Grabbing a pair of garden shears, she went to the cage and knelt down, positioning the shears against the metal wires.

"Get back, boy," she said through clenched teeth as she squeezed the shears and clipped through the first wire.

The metal broke and Emily exhaled in relief. Her breath came out in a cloud of mist.

Emily's stomach dropped. Consumed with rescuing Archie and making as little noise as possible, she hadn't noticed the significant drop in temperature.

It was practically freezing. She could even see that Archie was trembling within the crate. He whined and scratched at the corners of his confines, as if he knew something bad was coming. If Emily's theory was correct about Kat being connected to the ghost in some way, then this whole time Archie had been sensitive to, and much more aware of, the ghostly activity within the manor. She knew that it was thanks to him that she was even alive.

She *had* to get him out.

Determined and trying her best to ignore the frigid air, Emily began clipping the wires of the cage as fast as she could. With every snip, her hands shook harder, but she managed to get almost all the way around before the shears jerked in her grasp.

Her heart jumped with the tool, almost losing the shears entirely, but she managed to hold on tight. It felt like someone was trying to tear them from her grasp, as if there was actually another person—an invisible person—holding the blades and tugging them.

And then, with one great yank, the shears flew out of Emily's hands and smashed through the window, showering her with broken glass. Tucking her head under her arms, Emily couldn't stop a soft cry escaping from her lips. Archie growled next to her and then started to bark. At what, Emily couldn't see, but that wasn't her priority. If the ghost was here, she had to get Archie out before the ghost could do anything else.

Emily hoped that what she'd been able to clip would be

enough. She threaded her fingers through the wires and pulled as hard as she could. Miraculously, the wires started to bend backward, straining and trembling as she pulled harder.

Suddenly *all* the basement windows exploded. Glass shards rained down on Emily, and she screamed, tucking her head and her arms inward while still pulling at the metal wires.

She wasn't leaving Archie. The ghost would have to do better than that to scare her away.

With one final, powerful tug, she grunted, "C'mon, boy!"

Archie hunched his shoulders and wiggled through the opening, escaping from captivity and shaking himself like he'd just gotten a bath.

But Emily didn't have time to celebrate her friend's freedom. A cold breeze blew in from the windows, scattering the glass shards on the floor as a soft giggling echoed through the basement.

"Leave us alone!" Emily cried, stumbling toward the stairs and beginning to climb them. With Archie hot on her heels, they emerged into the scullery, and Emily whirled around, slamming the basement door behind them and locking it.

She knew a locked door wouldn't stop the ghost, but it made her feel a bit better somehow. But this was not the locked door that mattered. The only one Emily cared about in that moment was the door at the end of the third-floor west wing.

It was time to get the skeleton key and see what was hiding behind that lovely white door.

Before leaving the scullery, Emily took a moment to snag a scrap of meat left over from the fancy dinner and feed it to Archie. He gobbled it up and licked her fingers gratefully, which earned him a brief smile from Emily. After all, he deserved a treat for his time in the cage. Of course, he deserved an entire turkey for all that he'd done for her.

"Are you ready, boy?" Emily asked, bending down to scratch his ears and nuzzle his cheek against hers. She didn't want to ask him to come, but she knew he'd follow her. Either that, or he'd whine at being left behind.

Besides, if she was being completely honest, it was much too scary to go alone.

Together, they started through the quiet house. Apparently the glass shattering in the basement hadn't been loud enough to wake either the Thorntons or Miss Greer. Emily was quite sure that the ghost would come back for them, but it seemed to be biding its time, waiting for Emily to make another move. Or maybe the ghost simply enjoyed seeing Emily scared and anxious, watching her squirm.

It seemed like the kind of thing a spiteful, vindictive sort of ghost would like.

Clenching her jaw and steeling her nerves, Emily balled her hands into fists, and her footsteps became heavier—almost stomping down the hallways. She didn't like being toyed with or made fun of. She'd suffered enough of that at the orphanage from a live girl.

When she and Archie finally neared the Thorntons' bedroom on the second floor at the end of the east wing, Emily turned to Archie and pointed down. "Sit."

Archie sat obediently.

"Now stay," she instructed, holding out her palm as she slipped through their bedroom door.

Archie tilted his head and made a soft whine.

Mimicking Kat's actions, she pressed a finger to her lips and whispered, "Shh, boy."

When she was sure that Archie wouldn't come in or make any more noise, Emily turned back to the room. It was very large, that was for sure. At the front of the room near the door stood a tall armoire with a dresser, a vanity, and a full-length mirror. All were made from a deep red wood that looked shiny even in the low light of the moon coming through the large windows. The Thorntons slept in the biggest bed Emily had ever seen, with a canopy over them, the curtains pulled back and tied to the posts with gold cords.

Holding her breath, Emily quietly tiptoed past the furniture to the side of the bed where Mrs. Thornton slept.

Her adoptive mother slept on, but Emily could tell that she was restless. Her expression wasn't content—not in the least—and under her eyes she looked puffy and pink, swollen from crying. Her cheeks looked sunken. Maybe she hadn't been eating very well, or maybe Mrs. Thornton was haunted by something else. A secret from Blackthorn's past that no one would speak of.

The key to Blackthorn's past lay—literally—around Mrs. Thornton's neck. Emily was disappointed to find that, since the party, Mrs. Thornton had moved the skeleton key from her wrist back to its designated resting place at the base of her neck. This was going to be more difficult than she had anticipated.

Tongue between her teeth, heart racing, Emily reached over the edge of the bed and ever so carefully began to rotate the necklace to reveal the clasp. Mrs. Thornton made a small moan in her sleep and turned her head, which made Emily freeze in her movements, but she still slept on. Moving faster, Emily finally had access to the clasp and began to unhook it. Her fingers were shaking so hard it was nearly impossible to unclasp the chain, but as soon as the necklace fell limp and Emily grasped the key in her hand, the air in the room seemed to be sucked in, as if the entire house was taking a deep breath, then released it in one loud moan.

The moan came from all around them—the floor, the walls, the ceiling, the windows, the furniture. The entire house and everything in it seemed to be howling at Emily.

Suddenly the Thorntons sat upright in bed, their eyes wide and terrified.

Mrs. Thornton stared down in utter horror at Emily holding the skeleton key necklace in her hand. "Emily!" she gasped, extending her arm, reaching for the key.

Mr. Thornton gave a shout and jerked away from his side of the bed.

A figure appeared beside him—an angry figure Emily had seen before.

It was Kat.

# 18

Emily stumbled backward, away from the bed, still clutching the skeleton key tightly in her fist.

The image of Kat standing next to the Thorntons' bed was haunting. Kat's skin was deathly pale, her cheeks were sunken in, and there were large dark circles under her eyes. Her usual gold curly hair hung flat and tangled around her thin shoulders.

But her eyes were the worst of all. They were black as coal; even the whites around her eyes were gone. She stood there, not as a ghost, but as a walking corpse.

And that's when Emily knew: The girl she'd been playing with this whole time . . . *she* was the ghost.

Kat's jaw dropped open and the house moaned louder. The moaning increased until it became almost deafening. Mrs. Thornton slumped over into the pillows, fainting from fright. Mr. Thornton barely noticed his poor wife as he shuffled away from the girl, shaking with shock and terror.

"You shouldn't have done that," Kat hissed, her voice somehow next to Emily's ear even though she still stood on the opposite side of the bed. "How *dare* you try to take them away from me? How *dare* you try and make them *FORGET* ME?!"

With those words, the windows exploded all around them. Glass shattered everywhere, flying across the room and embedding itself into the carpet and the walls. Emily screamed and crouched down, throwing her arms over her head, too scared to run, too scared even to move.

Amid the chaotic scene, a bark came from behind her. Emily glanced over her shoulder and saw Archie squeezing his way through the half-closed door. He dashed to her side and faced Kat from across the bed, the hair on the dog's shoulders raised and his sharp canine teeth bared in fierce protection.

Kat glared at Emily, her black eyes narrowing into slits. Then the shadows that had been crawling down the walls slithered across the floor toward Kat, climbing over her feet and winding up her limbs like vines. Sludge coated the ghost girl, transforming her into a monstrous figure wrapped in a cocoon of living, evil shadows.

The house moaned again, louder this time, and the very floor shook beneath them. Next to Emily, Archie started barking like crazy, and even though Emily was too scared to raise her head, she could feel the monstrous ghost moving toward her, looming over the bed and the Thorntons, dripping with shadows and hate and rage.

The voice once again whispered in her ear as if she was right next to her. "You will never—*ever*—replace me."

As frightening as it all was, and as hopeless as it all seemed, Emily's head jerked up at Kat's words.

She stared at the monsterlike shadows inching toward her, though Archie's barking seemed to be keeping them at bay. Kat, wrapped in darkness, leaned over the bed, her jaw opened and the moaning growing ever louder.

"Replace you . . ." Emily repeated in a whisper, the gears in her mind slowly turning.

Emily stood, suddenly finding strength she didn't know she had, with the prospect of an idea—a nagging suspicion that she had been blind to since she'd arrived at Blackthorn.

Squeezing the key tightly in her hand, Emily spun on her heel and ran for the door, bursting out into the hall-way while Archie ran by her side.

At first, Emily wondered if she had escaped from Kat. She was running so fast down the hall that all she heard were the wind rustling in her ears and the heartbeat in her chest and the panting of her breath.

But then the shadows came.

They came from every direction. Sliding off the walls, emerging from the cracks, rounding the corners. They crawled toward her, moving fast and steady as if waiting for Emily to trip or run out of energy so they could grab her.

But cold, hard fear and a wild determination carried Emily's legs faster down the hall. The shadows kept chase, nipping and clawing at her ankles and the hem of her nightgown. One grabbed hold of the lace, and she could feel the chill set into her legs, but Archie snapped at it and the shadow whipped away. She cried out and ran on, Archie growling and snapping at the evil shadows as they raced down the hallways together.

They passed another room. Its door suddenly burst open and out flew an entire side table. The table whizzed right in front of Emily's nose, narrowly missing her, and smashed into the opposite wall. The table broke apart in a shattering blow of wood pieces as Emily lunged to cover Archie.

But there was no time to stop and be thankful that the table had missed them. The shadows bit at Emily's toes and brushed against her ankles. If she stayed in one place too long, she didn't doubt that eventually she'd be swallowed by them, and she didn't want to find out what lay within that darkness.

With Archie at her side, Emily jumped past the broken table pieces and continued running down the hall. It seemed to go on forever! Was this another ghostly trick as well? Would she ever escape?

Finally Emily came upon Mr. Thornton's study, right by the staircase. She was just able to glance inside when she saw a dozen books flying toward her at an impossible speed.

With a gasp, Emily dropped to the floor, flattening herself just in time as the flock of books sped through the air and crashed into the wall in a flurry of pages. As Emily got up, she recognized the deep red cover of the book *Alice in Wonderland* by her foot. The pages were ripped and the cover was torn, as though claws had sliced through the fine old leather.

Swallowing hard, Emily raced on, rounding the corner and up the staircase. Then the floor began to move under her feet. But it wasn't the entire floor, just the rug. It rippled and propelled her forward. Skidding on her knees, she tried to stand back up, but the carpet tripped her once more. The shadows, as if seeing their window of opportunity, hastened their chase and went after her.

Archie pounced on the rug, digging his paws into the fabric ferociously and biting at it with his sharp canines. Panting, Emily drew herself up and continued climbing the steps to the third floor.

"I want you to *GO AWAY!*" a voice said from above.

Scared to look up, but knowing she had to, Emily found Kat standing at the top of the staircase. She was Kat again. Not a dark, monsterlike creature covered in writhing shadows, but also not the Kat with whom Emily had played. This was the sickly Kat with snow-white skin, thin cheeks, and lank hair, as if she had been decomposing all this time.

"I'm not trying to replace you!" Emily called back. "I just want a home." Her voice broke—from either tears or terror, she wasn't sure. "I want a family."

"Well," Kat said, raising her hands, "you can't have *mine*."

Something above Emily's head snapped. It sounded like a chain breaking.

The great crystal chandelier that Emily admired came rushing down at her like a sparkling star falling to Earth. For one terrible moment, she was too scared to budge. Then Archie tugged at her hem, muffled growling rumbling from his throat, and Emily's feet began to move again. She ran up the stairs, breathless with fear and exertion as the chandelier collided with the steps, mere inches from where she was standing. Shards of crystal flew over the hall, the crash reverberating in her ears.

But Kat was momentarily gone. So Emily rushed up the remaining steps, turning down the west wing.

She couldn't stop. She couldn't give up. She had to end this.

The teeth of the skeleton key bit into her palm, digging grooves into her skin. The house moaned once again, and the hallway seemed to stretch impossibly long before her. She gritted her teeth and tried to run faster, but the scent of mildew and decay overwhelmed her. With her free hand she covered her mouth and nose. The wood and the moldings rotted before her very eyes. The spaces where portraits once had been were no longer white, but charred, as if the paintings had been burned away.

Another giggle came from next to her ear, and this time Emily did look. Kat was there, floating along beside her. She reached out a ghostly hand toward Emily, who ducked away, springing the last few steps to the pristine white door.

With quivering hands, she stuffed the skeleton key into the lock, and it fit perfectly. Emily turned the key and, mustering up every last ounce of strength she had, thrust her weight into the door—just as Kat's bitingly cold gray hand wrapped around her arm . . .

The door swung open and the hand on Emily's arm vanished. The moaning faded like an echo, and the freezing chill evaporated. The angry house seemed to settle like a rowdy child going down for its nap.

Still trembling, Emily took a few tentative steps into the room and looked around.

It was a bedroom.

A girl's bedroom.

It had white furniture with gold knobs on the dresser and vanity drawers. A mirror, similar to Mrs. Thornton's but smaller, stood in the corner, reflecting Emily, who stood still in her nightgown. The bed was white lace with gauzy curtains on either side. A braided pink rug and a white rocking horse with a pink-and-yellow mane sat in the middle of the room.

It was lovely. It was every girl's—no, every *princess's*—dream.

Slowly, Emily took a few more steps in, then gasped.

Kat suddenly appeared by the armoire. But she wasn't the ghoulish figure who had terrorized Emily that night. No, she looked . . . normal. Bright, healthy, in the pretty dress she always wore with her shiny shoes and golden curls. She didn't say anything, but instead looked sadly down at the armoire.

Knowing there had to be something significant there, Emily stepped forward, Archie still at her side, her ever-vigilant protector.

On the armoire, covered in a thick layer of dust, was a gold locket. It was a bit tarnished with age, but Emily could tell it was expensive and priceless to its wearer. The locket spelled *KAT*. It was the exact same as the one that hung around Kat's neck.

Emily looked up at the ghost girl with wide eyes.

"At least they didn't give you my room," Kat said sadly, her hands passing through the gold locket and the desk itself.

"Kat . . . I . . ." Emily tried to find words through the fear. Now that Emily knew she was talking to a ghost, everything she thought to say sounded insignificant in the face of death. How could she talk to someone who had *died*? How could she talk to her and comfort her when the very worst had happened?

Finally, Emily settled on the words she'd spoken in the hallway. Because they were the truth. "I never tried to replace you. I didn't even know about you."

Kat's bottom lip trembled, her fingers wiping away any tears from her eyes. "That's just it, isn't it? They don't talk about me, Emily. It's like I didn't exist at all. It's like they don't care about me, and they never did."

For the first time, Emily felt pity for Kat, and not for being a ghost, but for being just like her. A girl who felt unwanted. A girl who felt like she'd lost her home, or never had it to begin with.

“They locked my room and took down all my portraits,” Emily said, gesturing to the room. “All my dresses and dolls were put into the attic, and Miss Greer isn’t even allowed to say my *name.* They want to forget about me. It’s like I was never alive. It’s like I was never their daughter.” Her voice was a soft wail now, tormented and mournful, and Emily knew that this was what had started Kat on the path to becoming a vengeful ghost.

She was sad, lonely, and so very, very hurt.

Emily didn’t know what to say or how to comfort her. As the two girls stood there in silence, Emily noticed the light in the room slowly begin to change. From a room coated in shadows with glowing white furniture, it shifted into a room tinged with a soft orange-and-yellow glow as the sun slowly began to peek through the windows. In the light, Emily could just barely make out the blackberry bushes outside. The same blackberry bushes where she had met Kat.

“You can see the blackberry bushes from up here,” Emily blurted, without thinking.

Kat nodded. "Papa gave me this room so I could look out and tell when they were ripe for picking."

Kat loved blackberry picking, which is why it made the Thorntons so sad when Emily had come back with a whole pail of them.

They weren't trying to forget Kat because they didn't love her. They were trying to forget her because they loved her *so* much that every memory of her was painful.

Now that Emily thought back to her brief time at Blackthorn Manor, she could very clearly see the signs of Kat's existence. Even if Kat wasn't talked about in words, she was a constant presence in her parents' hearts.

"Kat, they *do* love you. They love you so much that it was painful to remember you, so they tried to get rid of everything that reminded them of you," Emily said softly, her voice growing stronger with every word, certain that she was right.

Mrs. Thornton had nearly started crying when she'd heard about Emily picking blackberries because Kat probably came home with them all the time. Miss Greer had told Emily not to play music because it was something that Kat had loved doing. Mr. Thornton had given Emily *Alice in Wonderland* because maybe Kat hadn't gotten the chance to read it.

Emily suspected they had picked her based solely on her appearance. Emily looked nothing like Kat. She was taller and had dark hair and dark eyes, while Kat was petite and blond with blue eyes. They were opposites in almost every way to make sure that when Mr. and Mrs. Thornton looked at Emily, they would not see Kat.

"I think they didn't want to cling to a past while facing a future without you in it." Emily sighed, looking around at the furniture that was so carefully built and beautifully painted. Clearly it was for a child they adored. "They miss you, Kat. This is how they've tried to move on."

Kat just looked at Emily, her shoulders slumped and her face still a little sad, but Emily could see a glimmer of hope in her eyes.

Then the ghost girl vanished, just as hurried footsteps

echoed down the hall, and both Mr. and Mrs. Thornton appeared in the doorway.

As the two looked around the room, their reactions were painful to watch. Tears started running down Mrs. Thornton's face immediately, and she clutched her hands to her mouth and nose. Mr. Thornton slumped against the doorframe, his face falling into defeat, exhaustion, and sadness.

"Katharine," he whispered softly.

Judging from their past reactions and all their attempts at shutting out their dead daughter from their lives, Emily knew she would be pushing them by asking about her. But it was the only way to convince Kat, once and for all, that she was still loved by her parents.

Swallowing hard, Emily took a few steps forward. "Is that the name of the girl who lived here? Your daughter?"

Mrs. Thornton sniffled while her husband stared at Emily, grief coating his features.

"Katharine Anne," Mrs. Thornton finally choked out amidst the tears. "Her name was Katharine Anne."

Katharine Anne Thornton. KAT. The initials on her locket.

"Yes." Mr. Thornton sighed heavily. "She died two years ago. We thought it was just a cold. But the coughing got worse and worse. She couldn't go outside anymore, and she was bedridden with an awful fever. We called for a doctor as soon as she started showing symptoms of consumption, but—"

"She wasted away so quickly," Mrs. Thornton struggled to say, her breaths labored with tears. "There was nothing we could do. Before we knew it, she was . . ."

Of course, Mrs. Thornton didn't have to finish. Emily knew all too well what had happened. She'd witnessed it happening to girls at the orphanage.

"We tried to move on, but the memory of her was too painful. Every day, we expected to see her come racing around the corner. So we tried to remove everything that reminded us of her," Mr. Thornton explained.

"But that's not moving on," Emily protested. "That's pretending the past never existed—that *she* never existed.

And I think that"—Emily paused, looking around the room—"that it would hurt her feelings to know you don't want to remember her."

Mr. Thornton's eyes widened. "Emily—"

"She's right, Robert," Mrs. Thornton said, shaking her head, her tears at last beginning to slow. "It breaks my heart to think that Katharine might not know how much we love her, or that we've tried to forget her. We need to stop pretending she was never here. Truthfully, her memory has haunted me. I feel like I see her everywhere."

Emily pursed her lips, not wanting to tell her that she actually had—that Katharine had, in fact, remained here as a ghost. On some level, Mrs. Thornton probably already knew that. Especially after last night's events.

Crossing to the armoire, Mrs. Thornton picked up the locket and wiped away the dust. "We should be celebrating the short time we had with her, not trying to forget it. Because it was precious." Then she threaded the locket through the chain that had once held the skeleton key and looped it around her neck.

Somehow, the room seemed to grow lighter with her words and her small gesture. Maybe it was simply the effect of the morning sun rising and spreading its beams into Katharine's room. But Emily suspected that it was more than that, because it was as if the entire house finally vanquished a heavy shadow that had loomed over it for so long.

# Epilogue

*One year later . . .*

Balancing a stack of books in her arms, Emily carefully made her way down the grand staircase. She could barely see the next steps over the tower of leather-bound novels, but she felt her way down them confidently. After going up and down them for an entire year, she knew which ones creaked and which were just a little bit higher than all the rest.

"Archie! Get back here!"

A blur of fur raced past Emily, making her books falter and teeter dangerously. Just as she was able to steady them, another figure came bounding down the steps and bumped her shoulder, spilling the books all across the stairs.

The maid spun around and gasped, her hands flying to her cheeks in almost comical embarrassment. "Miss Emily! I'm so sorry, I didn't see you!"

Emily couldn't help but laugh at the flustered new maid, Maggie. Her apron was twisted and her cap lopsided, while her cheeks were flushed. Maggie pointed down at Archie, who, at the bottom of the stairs, clutched a sponge in between his jaws and wagged his tail enthusiastically. "That rascal stole my sponge—it's the third one this week!"

Still giggling, Emily patted Maggie on the shoulder. "It's all right, Maggie, he just wants to play."

"Be that as it may, I still have a lot of work to do," Maggie harrumphed, folding her arms and tapping her foot.

Emily bent down and started to retrieve the books her father had lent her to read. "You've done so much work already, maybe you should take a day off."

It was true. With Miss Greer, Maggie, a butler, and two other part-time maids, the manor was well on the way back to its former glory. Every piece of furniture and corner of the estate had been scrubbed, polished, and dusted until it shined like crystal. Speaking of crystal, the chandelier had also been replaced with a new one. It was less extravagant, but the Thorntons agreed that they didn't need anything too fancy.

Emily glanced up at the big thing, remembering that not too many months ago the sight of it still scared her, along with the memory of it almost falling on top her. But now, the events of that awful night seemed like nothing more than a bad dream.

"Miss Emily!"

Emily looked down to see Miss Greer tugging the sponge from Archie's mouth. The housekeeper waved it irritably.

"The Mr. and Mrs. want you in the scullery," Miss Greer informed. "You're late!"

"I just wanted to put these books away," Emily called.

"I'll see to it, Miss Emily," Maggie said, taking the books from Emily's arms.

"Thank you, Maggie." Emily hurried down the steps, snapping her fingers at Archie. "C'mon, boy!"

Archie trotted after her happily. He'd enjoyed the extra staff as much as Miss Greer loved the extra help. He often played with them, hoping to get them to chase him around.

On the way to the scullery, Emily passed the portrait of a small blond toddler. She couldn't help stopping and smiling at the oil painting whenever she saw it. It was a lovely piece of art, but Emily admired it for other reasons.

Katharine Anne had been a beautiful child who filled the manor and the hearts of her parents with light. Now, three years after her death, portraits of Kat lined the hallways. This time, however, the memory of the young girl brought not painful feelings, but bittersweet ones.

Archie sniffed the air and whined, reminding Emily of

her destination. Scratching her friend's ears, they set off again down the hallway and emerged into the scullery to find Mrs. Thornton practically covered in flour.

"Emily, there you are! Come give me a hand, would you?"

A large mixing bowl sat on the big wooden table, and a whole mess of other ingredients were laid about its surface. Mrs. Thornton stood over the mixing bowl, struggling to stop the flow of flour from the large ten-pound bag she held in her arms.

Mrs. Thornton wasn't an excellent cook—or baker for that matter—but this was something she insisted on making herself every year.

Emily quickly rushed to her side and took the bag of flour and grunted, lowering it down to set it on the floor. Mrs. Thornton wiped her brow, leaving a white mark across her forehead, then placed her hands on her hips.

"Thank you, dear. I think we need milk next."

At that moment, Mr. Thornton came in bearing a pail of strawberries. "It'll have to be strawberries for the cake,

Charlotte. I looked high and low for blackberries but they're just not ready yet."

"That's all right, I suppose. Katharine always was the best at spotting the first few ripe ones."

"She'll like strawberry cake, too," Emily said, remembering the time that Kat had shown her the bunnies near the strawberry patch.

"Yes, I think you're right," Mr. Thornton said with a smile, kissing the top of Emily's head.

"Well, let's hurry it up, then," Mrs. Thornton said, gesturing for the strawberries. "This birthday cake isn't going to make itself!"

"Yes, we'll need to make this one fast so Miss Greer will have time to make another one," Mr. Thornton said, winking at Emily.

"And what is *that* supposed to mean, dear? Are you saying my cake will be inedible?"

"Nothing, darling. I just meant that yours is so good I'll eat it all myself and there will be none left for anyone else!"

Emily giggled as Mrs. Thornton swatted her husband with a mixing spoon. Though she could have sworn she heard someone else laughing, too.

That evening, after supper and cake time, Emily took Archie out for a brisk walk in the gardens. It was a lovely summer night, and the sun was just beginning to set over the grounds. She didn't have long to be out here before Miss Greer called her back in, but she enjoyed the time when all of the flowers smelled the best, right at sundown.

As she rounded a corner in the gardens, by the foxgloves and lavender, not far from the old well, she spotted a large pile of the ripest blackberries.

Before she even looked up, Emily knew who she was going to see. And she wasn't scared. She hadn't been for a whole year.

At the edge of the garden, near the blackberry bushes, stood Katharine with a big smile on her face. She lifted a hand, stained purple with blackberry juice, and waved.

Emily waved back, smiling.

The ghost turned and ran into the bushes, the tips of her gold curls disappearing in the yellow haze of the setting sun.

# Acknowledgments

I've always loved ghost stories. There was a time in my life when Betty Ren Wright and Mary Downing Hahn were my favorite authors. It feels like such a dream to be able to publish a book in the same space as theirs.

Of course, this could not have been possible without some amazing people.

To my agent, Frances Black with Literary Counsel, thanks for putting this deal together.

Orlando Dos Reis, my talented editor and all-around cool dude, thanks for believing in my writing and sharing my love of Victorian ghosts and phantoms.

What a delight it has been to work with you.

Thank you to the team over at Scholastic: Stephanie Yang, Yaffa Jaskoll, Caroline Flanagan, Courtney Vincento, Jackie Hornberger, Erin Slonaker, and Evangelos Vasilakis. Thank you to Scholastic Clubs and Fairs—a wealth of gratitude for this book and for making so many kids' days with your book fairs and flyers.

To my wonderful family—Mom, Dad, Jason, and Nichole—your support is much needed and much appreciated. And to my friends, you make ghost stories that much more fun to share. You know who you are.

# About the Author

Lindsey Duga is a young adult and middle-grade writer from Baton Rouge, Louisiana. Drawing inspiration from the cartoon shows and books she enjoyed as a kid, she wrote her first novel in college while obtaining a bachelor's in mass communication from Louisiana State University. *The Haunting* is her middle-grade debut. Her young adult fantasy novels include *Kiss of the Royal* and *Glow of the Fireflies*. Other than writing and cuddling with her morkie puppy, Delphi, Lindsey enjoys practicing yoga and ballroom dancing.